THE CALLING
OF
EMILY
EVANS

THE CALLING
OF
EMILY
EVANS
JANETTE OKE

JO

To those women
whose dedication and courage
opened many of the
community churches
for the Missionary Church
(formerly the Mennonite Brethren in Christ)
in the Canada West District.

JANETTE OKE was born in Champion, Alberta, during the depression years, to a Canadian prairie farmer and his wife. She is a graduate of Mountain View Bible College in Didsbury, Alberta, where she met her husband, Edward. They were married in May of 1957, and went on to pastor churches in Indiana as well as Calgary and Edmonton, Canada.

The Okes have three sons and one daughter and are enjoying the addition to the family of grandchildren. Edward and Janette have both been active in their local church, serving in various capacities as Sunday-school teachers and board members. They make their home in Didsbury, Alberta.

Table of Contents

Prologue

Although Emily Evans is totally fictional, the story she tells may well have happened. The Missionary Church was not the only denomination that sent young women out to pioneer new works in the Canadian West. It was not an easy task. There were times when they did not even have horses to help with their traveling. Many lonely and difficult hours were spent walking the dirt roads and paths in order to make calls on all the homes in an area.

But even when a mission worker was blessed with a team and buggy, her lot was not always that much easier, for often the roads were little more than winding trails through the countryside. And sometimes heavy rains or drifting snow made them nearly impassable.

Her accommodations were not that fancy either. Wooden crates stacked one on top of the other could comprise a good share of a room's furniture. Sometimes the girls boarded with an area family, but most often they were on their own.

The Sunday offerings were the workers' source of income. Many area farmers were good to share their farm produce, but in those early days on the prairies there was little extra to pass on to another household. The young women suffered the pioneering hardships right along with the families in the community.

In researching material for Emily's story, I scanned Conference Journals dating back to 1917, which for the Missionary Church was the twelfth annual conference. That would date the first conference as 1905, the year Alberta became a Canadian province. The efforts of the "Sister Workers" were reported along with those of the male ministers'. These reports included evangelistic meetings, tabernacle work, conducting the church services in local mission churches, working in a home established for unwed mothers, and "taking meetings over the needy prairies"—all done by "Approved Ministering Sisters," as they later were called.

In reports by women in the Journal of 1919, I saw references to the flu epidemic and concern for the returning soldiers of World War I.

The 1920 Journal tells of the committee appointed to decide the "uniform" of the Sister Workers: ". . . and that they dress in plain attire becoming to their work and the dignity of their calling, the wearing of low-necked waists [known to us as blouses or shirts] not being allowed, and the skirt must be ample in length and width." A simple dark bonnet was also a part of their dress.

Incidentally, the committee consisted of three women.

In the 1928 Conference of the Mennonite Brethren in Christ, held in Allentown, Pennsylvania, the presiding elder (later known as district superintendent) from the Canadian West field, Alvin Traub, reported to the conference: "Our preachers and workers are wholehearted and self-sacrificing and are devoted to their work."

I found twenty-eight names of Sister Workers listed in the early Conference Journals. Perhaps that does not seem like many, but, remember, in the beginning years of their ministry the Missionary Church had only three or four established parishes on these "needy prairies."

I recognized many of the names as those I had known as a child—missionaries, lady evangelists, college teachers, and wives of pastors.

I personally owe much to those dedicated young women, for one of them, Miss Pearl Reist, began the work in the community where I grew up. My home church, Lemont Memorial, is named in her honor. She married an area farmer, Nels Lemont, and continued as a supporter and ardent worker in the little church long after a minister was found for the congregation.

Another woman, Mrs. Beatrice Hedegaard, was the children's camp evangelist when I at age ten made my personal decision to commit my life to the Lord Jesus Christ.

Mrs. Alma Hallman, though in her mid-nineties, is still able to care for her own apartment, attend our local church, and chat with good humor and a great deal of insight about the happenings of the church over the many years of her involvement. She showed me her "papers" and her "button" and shared tales about the hardships and dedication of the women who served the Lord and the church in the early years of this century.

Only God knows the full extent of the cost to those who gave totally of themselves. And He alone knows the number of lives their ministry affected through the chain reaction resulting from that service. We do know that from many of these small mission works have come pastors, missionaries, and lay workers.

Most of the Approved Ministering Sisters have now passed on to their heavenly reward, but the product of their selfless ministry remains.

Chapter One

Training

Emily Evans lifted a slender hand and pushed back a wisp of wayward brown hair. She arched her back slightly to try to remove a kink in her tired muscles, then reached up to gently rub the back of her neck. Her whole body was protesting the position she had held for what seemed to be hours. She slid the opened book back and pushed away from the small wooden table, which was her desk. She was tired. Tired of studying. Tired of bending over the printed pages. Tired of trying to fit all the historical facts into her weary brain.

She lifted herself from the straight-backed wooden chair and walked to the window. Her left hand reached out to the lace curtain and lifted it back, allowing her to see the silent scene before her. Had it not been for the moon smiling down from overhead, she would have seen nothing but blackness. As it was, all she could make out was the outline of another building, looming dark and plain in the silvery light.

Emily knew the scene by heart. She had looked out upon it many times since her arrival at Gethsemene Bible School nestled in the western Canadian town of Regis. Not a large school, it was not known for its greatness. Only those interested in its teachings seemed to be aware that it even existed. Except for the town folk, of course. To them it was another way of adding to their coffers in the sale of produce toiletries and winter boots.

There were only four buildings on the small campus. The

main structure housed the two classrooms, the library, and the offices. The ladies' residence was to the right and the men's to the left. Behind the main building and centrally located between the dormitories was the small chapel. Emily wished she could see it from her window. It was the chapel that was dearest to her heart.

She turned silently from the dark window so she would not disturb the sleeping form in the bed across the small room.

"I've studied quite enough," she murmured quietly. "What I don't know will just have to be left unknown. I can't think one moment longer."

She looked at the sleeping form. *How can she breeze through the exams so easily?* was Emily's exasperated thought. *She never needs to study.*

Emily's dour assessment was not quite accurate. Ruth Raemore did study. But of course it was unnecessary for her to spend the time over her textbooks that Emily did. Though Emily was not brilliant, neither was she a poor student. Her high grades throughout her school days had resulted from disciplined hours of study. In Bible school, anxious to make the most of her years in training, she quickly found that diligent studying was the only way to make good grades.

The silence was broken by the unmistakable squeak of the second step of the stairs. Emily's head lifted, her breath catching in a little gasp. She did not hesitate to wonder who was making the silent ascent up those stairs and, then, down the hall. Each night the rooms were checked after "light's out," and Emily was tardy again.

As quietly as she could, she hurried across the distance between the window and the desk and quickly turned out her light. She could hear the quiet opening and closing of doors as the woman made her way down the line of bedrooms. With one swift movement Emily was out of her shoes and under the covers beside the sleeping Ruth.

Ruth stirred, turned over on her other side, and resumed deep breathing. Emily held her breath and made sure the covers were tucked snugly under her chin. Then turning her back to the door, praying inwardly that all of her long skirt had followed her under the quilt, she closed her eyes and waited.

Her door soon opened softly and with the light that filtered in from the hall, Emily could imagine herself being counted. Two forms in the bed. Two young ladies properly retired for the night. The door closed just as softly and Emily could sense, more than hear, the silent figure move on down the hall to the last room on the left.

Emily breathed again. She was saved from a scolding or more kitchen duty—at least for this time.

She dared not stir until she heard the footsteps descend the stairs. At last all was silent, and Emily folded back the covers and rose from the bed.

Now in the dark, Emily felt her way across the floor and removed the combs from her hair. She shook out the long strands, her fingers running idly through its silkiness. Tonight she didn't even stop to mourn the fact that her hair was plain— plain brown. Quite dark brown. How often she had looked at Ruth's raven black tresses, or Olive Tyndale's glowing blond crown, and longed for her hair to be such a color. But tonight she was too tired to care.

She stumbled over her kicked-off shoes as she felt her way to the clothes cupboard where her nightgown hung. She could not even see to properly hang up the clothes she had lifted over her head. She reached out and released them, hoping they were placed on the chair where she had been sitting. She wasn't sure if she heard them slide to the floor or not, but she did not feel for them in the darkness. She slipped into the printed flannel gown and carefully made her way back across the floor. The cold boards gave way to the braided rug, and she knew she had headed in the right direction.

Carefully she eased herself again into bed beside Ruth and snuggled into the warm blankets. She hadn't realized how chilly the room had become until she felt the warmth of the bed. Her sore muscles seemed to soak up the heat, and her head, now nestled on the pillow, began to ache in protest.

She chided herself. *I must start getting to bed earlier or I'll be sick again—just like Father warned.*

But even before Emily closed her tired eyes, she argued back.

But how can I? If I don't study, I'll never make it. They might not even let me stay. But if I don't go to bed on time . . .

Emily let that thought go unfinished. She knew there were good reasons for getting sleep. Her health depended upon it. She had never been physically strong. She was also breaking school rules, and at this small Bible school, rules were made to be kept. Emily chafed under the guilt that hung over her. What would they do with her if they ever found out that she was pushing "lights out" all too often? That she had bounded into bed on more than one occasion as she heard the preceptress's footfall on the stairway?

Emily shivered even in the warmth of the blankets. She did not welcome the thought of being sent home in humiliation. She wanted to be here. She had so much to learn. In a way that she couldn't explain, she felt compelled to study God's Word.

So why did she continue in her disobedience? Emily could only shake her head. "It's their rules," she mumbled, half asleep. "Nobody could live with such silly rules."

Ruth stirred again and Emily realized she had been pressing a bit closer than she intended in order to draw from the warmth. She shifted her body away and allowed herself to drift off to sleep. The rising bell would sound all too early, and everyone was expected to be at the breakfast table, properly combed, washed and dressed for another day in the classroom.

When the bell rang the next morning, Emily stirred restlessly and would have rolled over and gone back to sleep had not Ruth called, "Emily. Emily! It's time to get up. You'll be late for breakfast again."

Emily moaned and pulled the blankets a little higher.

"Emily! You told me not to let you sleep—remember?" Ruth scolded softly from in front of the room's only mirror. "Come on. You've got to get up."

When Emily still failed to respond, Ruth leaned over the bed and tugged the blankets from Emily's possessive hands.

"Emily!" Ruth said sharply.

Emily's eyes immediately flew wide open. Panic filled them

as she looked up into the dark-brown eyes of her roommate.

"What is it?" she asked, raising from her bed.

The sternness left Ruth's face and a smile turned up the corners of her lips.

"Nothing," she answered with a chuckle.

Emily flopped back to her pillow.

"Then what are you—?"

But Ruth did not allow her to finish. "It's past time to get up. You'll be late again. You asked me to be sure to get you up. Remember?"

Emily sighed. "Oh, yes," she admitted in a half whisper.

"Then get," urged Ruth, sternness back in her voice.

Reluctantly Emily sat up on the edge of the bed, and slowly rose to her feet to begin her morning preparations. The bathroom down the hall was shared by all the young ladies in the dorm, and Emily slipped into her robe and began to gather her toilet articles. Her eyes swung to the clock on the desk and she gasped.

"It's already ten to," she moaned. "Why didn't you get me up sooner?"

"I tried," said an exasperated Ruth. "How I tried! You are impossible to awaken in the morning. *You* ought to try it!"

Emily said nothing, grabbed everything she thought she would need and left on the run for the bathroom.

She was soon back, scrambling into her long gray skirt and fresh white blouse with the lace collar. Then she set to work on her unruly hair, running the brush through it as quickly as she could and fastening it up at the back of her neck. She hoped it would hold. Emily was often embarrassed by the hairpins coming out halfway through class. She poked in another pin as an extra measure of insurance, but even that did not make the roll feel any too secure.

Ruth was already moving out into the hall when Emily turned to follow.

The last breakfast bell sounded. At least she would not enter the dining room alone, in breathless fashion, while the rest of her classmates were ready to seat themselves. She cast one last look around her room.

She had tidied nothing after her return from her morning toilet. Her brush and comb lay on the desk where they had fallen. Her nightgown dangled haphazardly from the bed. Her dress from the day before reclined half on, half off the desk chair. Emily sighed deeply and resolutely hastened her step. She would have to do all her tidying after her morning kitchen detail and sometime before having her devotions. She would be expected to be on time for her first class—the one with the Bible History exam, and she had hoped to be able to spend a few moments in review.

Well, there most certainly won't be time for review this morning, she concluded reluctantly. She might even have to skimp on her devotions in order to get everything done. Emily hurried into the dining hall and was able to reach her assigned table in time for Carl Tyndale, Olive's blond brother, to hold her chair while she was seated.

"Good morning, Miss Evans," he whispered in a teasing voice. "I see we made it this morning."

Emily gave him a withering look. She wasn't quite ready for jokes.

"Shall we stand for the blessing?" came the voice of the preceptress. "Mr. Russell, would you lead us in the Grace?"

Emily stood and bowed her head. Subconsciously her spirit began to quiet, her soul to respond. Fred Russell always seemed so close to God when he prayed. Emily wanted that more than anything in the world. She wished with all her heart that she knew his secret. She strained to hear every word of the prayer above the quiet rustle of the dining room. A new calmness descended upon her as she began to sense the presence of God.

When she sat down again at the table, a new attitude possessed her. Her tiredness and anxiety seemed to disappear. She knew—she knew without a doubt what she was doing here in school. She knew what she wanted with her own life. She knew that no matter how difficult it might be for her to keep up with the studies and the multitude of scheduling bells, she was where she belonged. Where she needed to be. She longed with every fibre of her being to know God better, to understand His way, to find His will for her scattery life.

She sighed again—this time not in impatience and frustration but in longing. She lifted her eyes to face her fellow classmates around the table and gave them one of her lovely smiles. She was ready for the day now. She'd get her chore of dreaded pots and pans over in quick order so that she might properly tidy her room for morning check. Then she'd take the time to have a meaningful morning devotional time. What she didn't know for the exam would just have to be endured. She knew she needed God's presence more than high test scores, as important as she knew her studies to be.

And just as it seemed Emily's thoughts and day were well under control, she felt the hairpins give way at the base of her neck and knew that one side of her loosely held roll was spilling down her back. With a red face she excused herself from the table and went to re-pin her hair, firmly and properly.

Chapter Two

School Days

When Emily's Bible History test was returned, she was relieved to see that she had received a good grade. Excitedly she hurried off to her dorm room to share her wonderful news with Ruth. But Ruth was not alone when Emily bounced into the room. Olive Tyndale's blond hair was flowing freely down her back while Ruth snipped at the ends of the golden tresses with her blunt fabric scissors.

Emily slid to a stop. She could hardly just burst in, waving her test paper and boasting about the grade she'd received.

"—and do you know what he said to me?" Olive was saying. "He said, 'Your hair looks like spun gold.' That's what he said. I couldn't believe it." She gave a little giggle.

Ruth's scissors continued to snip. Her expression did not change. Olive was always spilling some secret comment of one young man or another. Ruth listened but paid little notice. She simply was not given to swooning over beaus, but if Olive wished to do so, that was her privilege. Besides, the compliment was certainly not very original.

"And then he said—"

"Emily," Ruth cut in, "Mary Friesen was looking for you. She said she had to go to the store for some shampoo and wondered if you would like to walk along."

"I would," Emily admitted, "but I just don't have the time. I have my report for tomorrow's Pentateuch class to prepare—

and I have resolved to get to bed on time tonight."

"Then maybe you should let Mary know. She's been waiting for you."

Emily went down the hall and rapped lightly on Mary's door, but it was Mary's roommate who called, "Come in."

"Ruth said Mary was waiting for me," Emily explained.

"She was," answered Pearl, "but she finally left. She has to be back for detail so she asked Liz to go with her."

Emily nodded.

"Is that your Bible History test?" asked Pearl, noticing the paper in Emily's hand.

Emily glanced at the paper she was still absent-mindedly holding and excitement filled her again. She nodded, trying to keep the pleased gleam from her eyes.

"What'd you get?" inquired Pearl candidly.

"Eighty-seven," answered Emily.

"Eighty-seven percent?"

Emily nodded.

"That's good," Pearl replied admiringly. "I got sixty-eight and I thought I did well. Even Fred got only eighty-two. That was a hard test."

For a moment Emily was swept with a feeling of pride. *I even beat Fred Russell!* she exulted. Then her instant glory faded away. Fred had not been able to study for the test. He had been called home because his mother was ill, and he had only arrived back on campus the night before the exam. Her pride quickly changed to sympathy for Fred.

"He didn't get to study—remember?" Emily reminded Pearl.

"I know," agreed Pearl. "Still, you did beat him—and rather handily, too."

"Well, it hardly—"

But already Pearl was changing the subject. "What are you wearing to the Missions dinner on Friday?"

"I don't know. I haven't even given it a thought."

"Are you being escorted?"

Emily shook her head. She still wasn't sure if she wanted to be escorted. The only fellow on campus that she really liked had invited Olive. Olive with her blond spun-gold hair. Emily had long since given up her secret dream that Ross Norris would ever notice her.

"No-o," she answered hesitantly.

Pearl sighed. "Max asked me, but I said no. So I guess I'm stuck with going alone." She sighed again. "I was really hoping Carl would ask me first. Now I won't be able to accept when he does ask."

Emily wondered why Pearl thought Carl would be asking her, but she didn't voice the question. Instead, she responded good-naturedly, "You can sit with me if you want some company."

Pearl nodded. "Thanks," she said. "I might."

Emily left to return to her own room. She had to get busy with her assignment. It would soon be time for the dinner bell.

Olive was still there. Ruth had completed the task of trimming her hair, but Olive had not bothered to re-pin it. Instead, she sat on the edge of the bed, running long slender fingers through the silken strands.

"—and Rob said that I shouldn't worry my pretty head about it," she commented coyly.

"Rob?" questioned Ruth without too much interest.

"Rob. Robert Lee. I call him Rob," answered Olive with a toss of the golden hair.

"You are supposed to call him 'Mr. Lee,' I believe," commented Ruth dryly.

Olive chuckled. It was school rules that the young men and women address one another with proper respect—not on a first-name basis.

"Oh, I do—whenever we're within earshot of one of the faculty," she assured Ruth, then cast a look toward Emily. "Are you going to study?" she asked incredulously as Emily cleared a spot on the crowded desk and arranged her books.

"I must," Emily answered. "I have an assignment to get done for tomorrow."

Olive sighed. Due assignments were such a bore.

"I need to get busy, too," Ruth informed Olive in a courteous but firm dismissal. Reluctantly the girl eased herself from the bed, still running her fingers through her hair, then tossed it back over her shoulders and picked up her hairpins and combs.

"Okay, Bookworms," she chided pertly. "Stick your noses back in your books." She left the room humming a popular song often played on the radio.

Emily settled herself at the small desk. "Do you need some room?" she asked Ruth, trying to figure out what she could move to give Ruth space on the one small surface.

"No, I think I'll go to the library. I need some reference books for my report."

Then Ruth noticed Emily's Bible History paper.

"How did you do?" she asked with interest.

Emily could not keep her eyes from lighting up. "Better than I thought I would," she enthused. "I got eighty-seven."

"Good," Ruth rejoiced with Emily. "From what I've heard, that's one of the higher marks of the class."

"Is it?" Emily could hardly believe that she was topping her classmates. She who always had to work so hard for her grades.

"Even Fred—" began Ruth.

"I know. Pearl told me. But Fred wasn't here to study," Emily said once more.

Ruth just nodded her head and gathered up her books with a "See you later."

From down the hall came Olive's giggle followed by a little shriek from Pearl. Olive had not returned to her room to prepare for the next day's classes. She and Pearl were likely exchanging stories about the cute things that the young men on campus had said to them recently.

Emily bent over her book and set her mind to studying—but the words seemed to blur before her eyes. Through her mind ran the catchy little tune Olive had been humming. No matter how hard she tried, the tune insisted on going round and round in her head.

Oh, bother! fumed Emily. *I might as well have gone up town with Mary. I can never study with all the commotion.* She concluded that she would never get in step with dorm living. Waiting for late-night quiet seemed to be her only recourse.

But Emily did eventually get into her report. She even became so engrossed that she missed the warning dinner bell and might have missed dinner had not Ruth arrived back from the library to inform her that they must rush or they would be late. Emily pushed back her books and rose to follow Ruth. In her hurry she bumped some papers from the desk and stopped to retrieve them. Ruth's Bible History test had big red markings giving her score. She had made ninety-two percent! Emily's eyes widened.

"And without any effort," she muttered to herself. Suddenly she felt that life was not fair.

Then she hastened from the room and ran the few steps down the hall to catch up with the other girls. Nobody had ever said that life was fair, she told herself, and besides, if anyone deserved it, Ruth did. Emily pushed her agitated feelings from her with determination. She refused to be jealous over her roommate's ability. God expected Emily Evans to do only what she was capable of doing. No more—and no less.

Chapter Three

Classmates

Emily found that it was all she could do to accomplish her assignments in time for the next day's classes. On more than one occasion she broke the lights-out rule, though she didn't intend to do so. And she was occasionally still late for breakfast—in spite of Ruth's insistence that she must get up. But Emily tried. She honestly tried to keep up with the demands of the school. It seemed to her that she was always rushing, always pressing, always scurrying to keep up with the rest. Yet in all of the hurry, she was conscious of a strange serenity that she was in the right place, doing the right thing. Her knowledge of the Bible continued to grow daily.

To Emily the most special time of the day was the chapel hour. She loved to hear the hymns as the students joined in singing, the men on one side and the women on the other. She thrilled with the testimonies of fellow students. She drank in the preaching hungrily. There was *so much* she longed to know. She felt unworthy to be at such a place of learning—yet deeply thankful that God had allowed her to come.

Not all of Emily's activities were serious and studious. She enjoyed the parties held in the dining hall. Skating was allowed at the local pond. Interaction was encouraged, though formal dating was limited. But during the school year the young men and women became acquainted in a proper and chaperoned environment. Emily soon learned to identify each of her classmates, not by name or appearance, but by personality traits.

As far as Emily was concerned, Ruth was the perfect example of what a young Christian woman should be. Though rather plain in appearance, perhaps, she was alert, capable, intelligent and devout. Her no-nonsense approach to life fit well with her deep desire to serve the Lord. Emily thanked God many times for giving her a roommate like Ruth.

Olive, the one with the pretty hair, was flighty, flirty, and seemingly out-of-place at a Bible school. *But perhaps God has His own reasons for bringing her here,* Emily concluded.

Mary, quiet and studious, asked little of others and gave much in return. Emily found Mary easy to love. She was of the stuff that close friends were made from.

Though not as enamored with the opposite sex as Olive was, Pearl was certainly more attractive, and she didn't pretend not to know that young men occupied the same campus. She was quick to laugh and witty in her responses. In a way, Emily could have easily envied Pearl.

One by one Emily mentally reviewed her dorm sisters. They came from many backgrounds, looked quite different, had varying personalities, but they shared many things—besides the large common bathroom with its curtained showers and stalls. They shared dreams and hopes and aspirations. They shared a desire to study the Word and to share that Word in some way with others. At least, *most* of them were on campus to study and grow.

Emily was also aware of the young men on campus, though not nearly as much so as Olive and Pearl. Carl Tyndale, blond like his sister, was the campus tease, the one who was usually thinking of some silly prank to pull on an unsuspecting fellow student. Occasionally there were whispers of Carl being sent home if he didn't conform to the school standards of conduct, but the days passed by and Carl remained. Emily thought the dean was patience personified when it came to his dealings with Carl.

To Emily, Fred Russell was as much the example for the men as Ruth was for the young women. A spiritual leader, he was studious, sensitive, committed and deeply respected. The faculty counted on Fred to set the tone of the school. One could not dislike Fred. It would have seemed near to blasphemy.

Robert Lee, known to Olive as "Rob," was the campus flirt, or so Emily thought. He may have told Olive not to worry her pretty little head, but he told every girl on campus some such silly rubbish. Emily paid little attention to the cute sayings of Mr. Lee.

Morris Soderquist, his heavy glasses framing deep blue eyes, was a slight, wiry young man with a deep sense of commitment to his goal. He intended to go overseas to the mission field, and he pored over his Bible with intensity as he prepared himself for service. Conversations with Morris were few and far between, for he was always in the library or in his own room studying.

Lacey Beckett, a big farm boy, was tall and heavyset. His voice matched his appearance and his laugh rumbled through a room. Emily felt that fate—or whatever or whoever was responsible for naming Lacey—had somehow played a cruel trick. The name simply did not fit the man. Lacey was anything but fragile or feminine. Emily had to keep herself from giggling every time she heard or read his name. She was glad she had to call him "Mr. Beckett"—she was sure she could not hide her amusement if she were to call him "Lacey."

Thirteen young men in all filled the men's residence. Each one added a personal dimension to the student body and, together with the fifteen young ladies, formed a unit of learning and growing, each contributing in some sense to the other.

———

Emily went home for Christmas to share some special times with her father and two sisters. Emily had been twelve when her mother was taken from them. Being the middle girl in the family, Emily had nearly been overlooked in the changing household. She had not had to take on the home duties that fell on Ina, nor was she petted and pitied like younger Annabelle. Only her father, who had always seen Emily as the most like her mother, had carried a special spot for her in his heart. Her rather frail body was his constant concern. Slight of stature and subject to flus and colds, Emily often carried out her responsibilities by sheer determination.

But Christmas had been a good time for all. They went to Grandma Evan's on Christmas Eve and to Grandma Clark's for Christmas Day. Ina was spared the burden of preparing a Christmas dinner, and Annabelle, now thirteen, was fussed over sufficiently to carry her through the months ahead.

Though Emily enjoyed Christmas, she secretly longed to get back to school. But she tried not to let her restlessness show, for she could feel her father's thoughtful gaze upon her. There was little chance for the two of them to talk privately, so Emily answered all the general questions about the school, her work, and her health. She thought she had given a satisfactory report until one night when she sat reading her Bible after Ina and Annabelle had retired.

A rustling of paper preceded her father's question. "How's school?"

"Fine," Emily answered simply, her eyes not leaving the page.

There was a moment of silence.

"How's school?" her father asked again.

This time Emily lifted her eyes and looked directly into his warm brown ones, now crinkled with interest and concern.

"Fine," she answered evenly. "I like it."

He nodded and his work-worn hands laid the newspaper in his lap. "You've been keeping well?"

Emily was about to nod in agreement when she remembered a bout with the flu that had kept her in bed for three days, and the last cold that bothered her for a week.

"Mostly," she said honestly.

"Are you takin' your cod-liver oil?"

The very mention of it caused Emily's pert little nose to wrinkle up, but she nodded vigorously.

"Good! You look a little peaked."

"Peaked" was one of her father's favorite words. He referred to any one of his children as being "a little peaked" whenever illness struck.

"I'm fine," Emily insisted.

"Got a good roommate?" was the next question.

"Ruth. She's great. I really like her. I just wish I could be more like her," Emily said sincerely.

"Nothin' wrong with you," her father was quick to assure her, and Emily flushed with the simplicity of his appraisal.

"Any special fellas?" asked Mr. Evans, and Emily's head lifted in time to catch the twinkle in his eyes.

She smiled slowly, then shook her head. She knew that Ross really didn't count. He still seemed to be carrying a torch for Olive, even though Olive responded positively and then ignored him, by turn.

She shook her head. "No one special to me—in that way," she admitted.

"Will Pearson still asks about you," Mr. Evans said, causing Emily to blush. Will Pearson had been asking about Emily for too many years. He was much older than she—nine years, in fact, and he had been living with false hope for a long time. Emily had no interest in Will Pearson, even if he did own his own farm.

"He thinks it a bit foolish that I favored you gettin' Bible learning. Seeing as how girls aren't preachers and all."

Emily lifted a stubborn chin. "Some girls are," she argued, as though Will Pearson were right in the room. "We've had women in chapel who are. They came with their preacher husbands. Both of them. Mrs. Witt, the district superintendent's wife, she can preach, too."

Mr. Evans looked surprised. "Women preachers? Never heard of it."

"Well, you can just tell Will Pearson the next time he asks that there *are* women preachers—aplenty."

Emily's chin lifted higher. What right had Will Pearson to dictate the role of women anyway?

Mr. Evans was quite intrigued by the news. "Ordained?" he asked, and Emily had to quickly think about what he was asking.

"No," she answered slowly. "Not ordained. But they preach—and they help in the church. And they lead people to the Lord, too."

"If they aren't ordained, how can they run a church?"

"They have a special—a special position. The denomination even gives them papers. It says right there that they are approved to minister."

"Do they do everything? Everything that a man preacher does?" queried her father.

"No-o," Emily had to admit. "They can't do things like marry or bury. Or baptize. Things like that."

"But they preach?" queried her father, scarcely believing that a woman could be placed in such a role.

"They preach," Emily assured him. "Mostly when their husbands have to be away. But Rev. and Mrs. Jackson—they take turns, Sunday by Sunday."

It seemed preposterous to Emily's father. "Well, I don't guess I'd care much to have a daughter of mine bein' a preacher— even if her husband was," went on Mr. Evans. "Seems to me that one preacher in a household is quite enough." He thought for a moment and then spoke again, quietly. "Not sure I'd want to be listenin' to a woman either, come to think of it." Emily wasn't sure if the words were meant for her or were just a quiet expression of the way her father felt.

"I think—I think—" and then Emily hesitated. Was she breaking a confidence? Her father looked at her, waiting for her to go on.

"I think Ruth might like to be one," she said at last, speaking barely above a whisper. "She hasn't said so yet, but she loves to study and says that she would love to preach. She just wants to teach and preach. She can hardly wait for her turn to share in chapel or at prayer meetings."

But Emily's father was shaking his head.

"Must be a strange one," he observed and then rose from his chair, signaling that it was time for them to put out the light and retire for the night.

Chapter Four

A Call

Emily arrived back at school with new resolve. She had no intention of going home to Jamestown and marrying Will Pearson—whether he was still waiting for her or not!

Several times she recalled the conversation with her father and realized that she did not share some of her parent's views. She believed a woman could join with her husband to serve in the role of church leadership. Emily began to secretly think that she would be honored if the Lord would favor her with a preacher-husband so that they could serve Him together. She began to look at her male classmates in a different way. Which ones would make good preachers? Which ones might answer a call from God to serve? Emily had never evaluated fellows in such a fashion before. But as she observed, she soon became convinced that Ross, for all his good looks and magic charm, would *not* be the man for her, even if he hadn't been smitten by the elusive Olive. Ross just was not preacher material, in Emily's estimation.

Carl was a bit too unsettled, a bit too frivolous to make a preacher. Fred, of course, would make a first-rate preacher—but Fred already had a lady friend by the name of Agatha. And comparing Fred with herself, Emily felt inadequate and lacking in spiritual depth. She would never be able to measure up as Fred's wife. She wondered silently if Agatha could.

Robert was not even considered a possibility. He was just

too silly—too insincere. Emily was sure that even God would be hard put to make much out of Robert.

Morris was headed for the mission field—and by all appearances he planned to go alone. Morris did not even seem to realize that girls were a part of the world.

Lacey, with his huge frame and boisterousness, was easily scratched from Emily's list as well. God would have to do a lot of polishing before Lacey could be ready to serve Him.

One by one each of Emily's fellow students was assessed and found wanting in one area or another. There just didn't seem to be anyone in her class who was right for Emily. Oh, she certainly knew young men with sterling qualities, but those whom Emily might have selected were already attached to someone else, or had stated their intentions of going back to the family farm or on for secular training. Emily couldn't see much future for her in the current prospects.

Yet the insistent desire to serve the Lord continued to fill her thoughts. "What can I do, Lord?" she kept asking in her daily prayers. "I have no place of service, no particular skills, and no one with whom to share a call."

In her devotional reading, scripture passages such as "Calling the twelve to him, he sent them out two by two" seemed to leap off the page and burn themselves into her heart. *What did it all mean?*

Emily did not wait patiently for the answer. She chafed inwardly, posed hard questions in class, sought counsel from fellow students, and listened intently in the worship services.

It wasn't until her first Bible school year had almost ended that Emily received her answer. Rev. and Mrs. Paul Witt, the district superintendent and his wife, were visiting chapel. Emily sat on the edge of her seat, her hands clasped into nervous knots in her lap, her hazel eyes opened wide with intensity.

"We have countless areas open to us," Rev. Witt was saying. "Places where they are begging us to come and start a church, and we have no one to send. God does not call us to sit idly by while the people perish. He has called us to go—to give—to preach the Gospel."

Emily could not help stealing a glance at the men's side of

the chapel. Surely many of them would be profoundly moved and anxious to answer the call to serve.

"We need to be willing to obey His voice as He speaks to us. Where are the men who are willing to bridge the gap—to answer, 'Here am I. Send me'? For how can they hear without a preacher? How can they preach except they be sent? We, as a denomination, are here to send you forth. We are here to back and support you. We are here to help you to obey God's call—to take up your cross and follow Him."

Is he speaking only to the men here? The question suddenly flashed through Emily's mind. She looked around her and caught Ruth's eye, then turned her attention back to the speaker.

"I urge you, if He is speaking to your heart, obey His voice—follow His leading today. Come. Come acknowledge His call on your life. Come forward and kneel here at the altar of prayer. Offer up your life as a sacrifice of love and obedience to the Lord who loves you. Who died for your salvation. Come. That others too might know the joy of knowing God."

Fred Russell was the first to move forward. Morris Soderquist was close behind him. And then, to Emily's surprise, Lacey Beckett was moving quickly toward the altar, tears on his round cheeks.

And then Emily could bear the intensity of the feeling in her heart no longer. With a sob in her throat, she hastily rose and practically ran to the altar railing where she knelt down and unashamedly buried a tear-streaked face in her clasped hands.

The answer had come. If God had no helpmate with whom she could share His call, she would go alone. It was as simple as that. Will Pearson might think it impossible for a woman to preach, but Emily knew otherwise. Hadn't she heard God's call? Hadn't He promised all of His children that He would be with them? Of course! Of course God could call a woman to serve. Emily had no idea just where and how—but she did know that her heart yearned to be of service to God.

"Yes, Lord. Yes," she prayed silently. "I'll go. Wherever you want me—I'll go."

A strange peace settled over her heart. She had been obedient. She was committed to Christ and to the goal of serving Him. She was only a girl, but God would be with her. He would lead her. Emily was sure of that.

Emily later learned that she had not been the only young woman at the altar. Ruth had, as Emily would have expected, joined those at the altar as well. Ruth, too, had answered God's call to serve Him—maybe even to preach.

After the altar service was over, the good Rev. Witt spoke softly to those who had stepped forward. As Emily lifted her swollen, red eyes and looked shyly about her, she was surprised to see seven of her classmates on the front benches.

Rev. Witt went slowly down the row, speaking to each person by name.

"Why are you here, Mr. Russell?"

Fred answered without hesitation. "I feel called to serve."

"And where would God have you serve?"

Fred shook his head. "It matters not," he answered just as firmly. "I will serve wherever my church places me."

The district superintendent smiled and nodded in agreement.

"And you, Mr. Soderquist?" he went on.

"God called me to the mission field when I was a boy," answered Morris with a trembling voice. "I came forward today to publicly testify to that calling."

Again the superintendent nodded.

"And you, Mr. Beckett?"

But Lacey Beckett could not readily answer. He was still weeping with the enormity of his conviction that he was called to serve.

Rev. Witt passed on. Emily felt a quiver go all through her body. She was next.

"What about you, Miss Evans?"

"God has called me to—to serve Him—somewhere—in some—some new church. I—I don't know where," Emily responded.

"God will show us where," the good man said with confidence, and the tears streamed down Emily's face again. She had been accepted. As simply as that, she had been accepted to minister for the Lord, to preach.

The superintendent heard testimony from each of the other students. Occasionally he stopped to praise God or to wipe his eyes with his handkerchief before continuing on.

Emily was filled with emotion at the intensity of this time. Surely great things would happen as a result of the day's chapel service. Eight more servants! Eight more to serve her God!

And then the service was dismissed and Emily was free to embrace her roommate and share in the excitement of being *called*.

———

All that week Emily walked on air. She was actually going to serve God in a new work—somewhere. Even now she was preparing herself for that service. She would prepare herself well. She needed to thoroughly know the Word. She would be sharing that Word with hungry people Sunday after Sunday.

And then, unbidden, a new thought came to Emily. She remembered the late nights—the stolen minutes after lights out and the jumping into bed under false pretenses to fool the preceptress. Surely God could not honor such actions. She was smitten with conviction, and tears stung her eyes. She had to make things right before she could go one step further. She had to confess her sin and ask for forgiveness. *Maybe they will refuse me an assignment someplace when they know how deceitful I've been*, she thought, her heart constricting with fear.

Reluctantly Emily placed one heavy foot before the other as she made her way to the office of Miss Herrington. She dreaded the stern look she no doubt would encounter in those sharp gray eyes. She could picture the pointed nose lifting slightly, and the lips pursed in a thin, tight line, expressing displeasure. Miss Herrington was a kind, godly woman, but Emily knew the preceptress did not have much patience with disobedience. Timidly Emily knocked at the door and was told to enter.

"Miss Herrington?" she addressed her dean hesitantly.

"Miss Evans," the woman responded, smiling pleasantly. "Come in. Do come in."

Emily closed the door behind her.

"You can't imagine how pleased we all are that you have presented yourself for service," the woman went on, beaming at Emily.

Emily's smile was shaky in return.

"Well, yes, I—"

"Have you had the opportunity to share your good news with your family?"

"No-o," Emily admitted and again remembered the discussion with her father. She wondered if her father would deem the "call" good news.

"You haven't written?"

"Well, no-o. I'm to go home this weekend. I thought that I'd rather—rather tell them firsthand."

The preceptress smiled. "Of course," she said. "It is always nicer to share those things in person."

The woman looked searchingly at Emily and seemed to sense that something was troubling her.

"Can I be of help in some way?" she asked solicitously.

Tears gathered in Emily's eyes.

"I—I have a confession," she admitted.

The smile left but the eyes still held softness.

"Go on," the woman urged.

"I—I haven't always been to bed on time. I—I mean I have studied after—after lights out. I—I'm rather slow—I mean in my studies. I need to spend much longer studying than Ruth, and so I—I—"

Then Emily finished lamely, "I broke the rules."

"But your light was always out when I came around for bed check," the woman puzzled.

Emily's face felt hot. "I—I would put the light out when I heard the stair step squeak," she admitted.

There was a moment of silence.

"I see," said the preceptress slowly.

"And—and on occasion, I—I got back up and put the light on again—after all was quiet, so I could study some more,"

Emily admitted. "I—I even laid my rolled-up towel at the door to cover the crack."

More silence. Then Miss Herrington commented, "I have watched your grades. You have been doing well."

"But I wouldn't have—without studying," Emily assured her, her words tumbling over each other. "I have always found learning more—more difficult than some. Even in grade school I had to work harder than Ina or even Annabelle—my sisters. I—"

"Miss Evans," the preceptress interrupted softly, "do you understand why we have the 'lights out' rule?"

"Yes." Emily's voice trembled.

"Why?"

"So that we get the proper rest."

"Correct. Lights out is not some casually contrived policy. Lights out is for your benefit. But that is not all. It is for the benefit of the total student body—so that you do not pass on an illness to the rest. You are cheating yourself when you break the rules. And perhaps endangering your fellow students."

Emily had not considered that before.

"You have been remarkably free of sickness this winter— but your faculty has been praying for you week by week."

Emily's eyes widened. She had no idea that her health was the subject of faculty prayers.

"Perhaps God has seen fit to answer those prayers in spite of your disobedience." Miss Herrington's gentle tone took some of the sting out of the words. "Because—because," she went on, "He saw a girl who wanted to get all she could from her studies."

Emily blinked.

"But," continued the preceptress, "one should not press, or be presumptuous, with God."

Emily wondered if the preceptress had been on the verge of saying "press one's luck." In spite of her mortification over the interview, she found it hard to suppress a smile.

"From now on, I shall expect you to be in bed at the proper hour."

"Yes, Miss Herrington," agreed Emily in a subdued tone.

"If you need to have more study time, we will try to find

some other way for you to manage it."

The kindness and consideration of the older woman surprised Emily. She had not expected such understanding.

Emily's eyes brimmed again. She felt more chastised than if she had been assigned further kitchen duty or soundly scolded for her crime.

"I am sorry—truly, I am," she sobbed. The woman offered her a clean handkerchief and Emily murmured her thanks.

"Miss Evans," the preceptress said, "you realize that if you had not come to me about your disobedience and I had discovered it another way, I could not have avoided disciplinary action."

Emily nodded and wiped her eyes, greatly relieved that she had been moved to seek forgiveness.

Miss Herrington reached out and patted her hand.

"Let's hear nothing more about it," she stated matter-of-factly, and Emily knew she had been dismissed. Dismissed and forgiven. Feeling a load had been lifted from her heart, she slipped from the room. She had not been condemned. She had not been removed from the list for future service. With great relief, Emily went back to her room to wash her face.

"Now if only Father will understand about my call . . ." she said under her breath and reached for her towel and washcloth.

Chapter Five

Sharing the News

Spring was knocking at the back door of winter when Emily stepped off the train at Jamestown station for her weekend at home. Here and there a bird twittered in expectation of warmer days. Bits of hardy green showed in small patches against the southern side of buildings where the snow had been forced to give way by warm sunshine. Emily took a deep breath and smiled her anticipation of milder weather, which she yearned for. Her health was always much better in the summertime.

If I go home with a bounce to my step and a healthy glow on my cheeks, Father won't be quite so hard to convince, she had reasoned to herself on the train ride home.

But even with those positive thoughts, Emily wondered.

Just how would her father accept the news of her "calling"? Besides his feeling regarding women preachers, he had inferred that Emily needed a hardy, solid man to care for her, to protect her from the strains that life often imposed. That probably was why he considered Will Pearson a good candidate. It was true that Emily's shoulders were not broad, nor her frame strong. *But God has other strengths He gives His servants,* Emily reasoned.

Emily's father greeted her at the station. She could feel his eyes scan her quickly. *I'm glad I had my coat properly buttoned,* she thought to herself. Then her glance followed his to her feet. She had neglected to wear her overshoes again.

43

"The streets were quite clear in Regis," she said defensively. "I didn't even think to wear my—"

He just nodded, his face solemn, as he reached for the small valise she carried. Emily knew he was not pleased with her carelessness.

She circled a spring puddle and had to run a few steps to catch up to her father, who had splashed directly through with his farm boots. She sought for something to say, but she couldn't think of anything except, "How are Ina and Annabelle?"

"They're doing good. Ina's fixin' supper and Annabelle wasn't home from school yet, so I came by myself." They lapsed again into silence.

When they reached the team and wagon, her father nodded for her to get in while he placed the valise on the floor boards. Emily climbed stiffly over the wheel and settled herself for the ride.

They were almost home before her father said, "How's school?"

"Fine," responded Emily, continuing to watch a distant V of returning Canada geese.

There was a moment of silence, and then her father spoke again.

"How's school?"

Emily jerked to attention. Her father had always used this device with his children. If they answered absent-mindedly, he simply repeated the question until they gave it proper consideration.

Emily's heart began to pound. *Is now the time to tell Father about my call?* She took a deep breath and decided to get it over with. Perhaps then they would have the rest of the weekend to sort it through—work it out.

"We had a wonderful chapel service recently," Emily began with a deep breath. "The Witts were there, and Rev. Witt spoke about the need for church workers. Then he gave an altar call. He asked those who felt God was calling them to serve Him to step out and come forward."

Emily stopped for breath—and courage. "Eight students went forward."

She hesitated again.

Her father had been watching her face as she spoke, and Emily turned to him now. She saw his eyes were alight and he answered almost under his breath, "Praise God."

Emily was pleased with his response. She knew her father was deeply interested in enlarging their mission of reaching local communities, particularly ones that had no church.

Emily took another deep breath and then blurted out hurriedly before the gleam left her father's eyes, "I was one of them."

A startled look passed over his face. Emily waited for the lecture to begin. There was nothing. Only silence. His eyes shifted back to the team he was driving. One foot stirred restlessly on the wooden boards of the wagon. Emily could see his hands tighten on the reins.

Still he did not speak. He had just thanked God that young people had been called to preach. And now he had to face the giving of his own flesh and blood—and one not too strong at that.

At length he nodded—just nodded his head in acknowledgment. He could hardly take back his expression of praise to God. But Emily could see the uncertainty in his eyes.

"Where?" was his simple response.

Emily shrugged her slim shoulders. "I—I don't know where—yet. Rev. Witt said that—that God would show us where."

He seemed to relax then. "You know you're not very strong," he began gently.

Emily's chin came up. "Scripture says that God often chooses the weak things to confound the strong," she reminded him.

He nodded, his expression saying there was no use arguing against Scripture.

They rode in silence again. Emily could tell that her father was mulling over the news. Finally he spoke again. "So who's the young man?"

Emily did not understand. "The what?" she asked.

"The man. When you were home at Christmas, you told

about a preacher and his wife both servin' together. I don't recall your writing about someone special. I would like to know the man my daughter will be sharing her life with. Who will you be goin'—"

"Oh," cut in Emily quickly, "I—I'm not interested in anyone. I'm quite prepared to go alone."

This did bring a sharp reaction from her father. "Alone?" he thundered. "That's absurd. You can't just go off and run a church alone. A young girl like you—sickly and—"

"I'm not sickly," Emily protested. "I've much more strength than you credit me with, Father. And I will have God to—"

"It's unheard of," her father continued, paying little attention to Emily's arguments. "It wouldn't even be decent for a young woman to be on her own. To try to manage a church. How can the district superintendent even consider such a thing? I won't hear of it! Not for one of my girls."

Emily bit her tongue. Now was not the time for the discussion to continue. Tears stung her eyes, but she wisely made no further comment. Inwardly she prayed. Prayed that He would speak to her father. If she was to answer God's call, He would need to convince her father that it was proper and right for a young woman.

"We'll talk later," he said at last, patting her arm a bit stiffly and flicking the reins to hasten the team.

He needs time to think—to pray, Emily concluded.

It was not until Mr. Evans was driving Emily back to catch her train that the subject was broached again.

"You know you are often ill," he began softly.

Emily nodded in silent agreement. It would have been foolish to try to deny it.

"You know that directing a church is hard, hard work."

Emily nodded at that as well.

"Why don't they send out two women together?" he demanded.

"There aren't enough of us to double up like that," Emily tried to explain.

"You'll likely spend many hours alone."

"I know," whispered Emily, the tears threatening to come.

"You'll have no one there to lean on."

"God will be there," Emily insisted in a trembling voice.

The plodding of the team, the creaking of the wagon wheels, and the occasional twitter of a bird were the only intrusions on the silence.

"And you still wish to do it?" Emily's father finally asked.

Emily turned pleading eyes to him. The tears clung to her lashes and she swallowed the lump in her throat.

"It is not what I want that is important," she murmured in a whispery voice. "I have been called, Papa. To disobey would only bring heartache. I must—I *must* answer my call."

She called him Papa only at very intimate times. It was what her mother had often called him. "Go ask your papa," the girls would be told. Or, "Call your papa for dinner." He turned his face slightly to hide his deep emotion. After a time, he cleared his throat and turned back to Emily.

"Then by all means, be obedient," he said huskily. "I—I will do—whatever I can to help."

With a glad little cry Emily leaned against her father and took his large hand in both her small ones.

"Thank you, Papa," she said through her tears. She knew her prayer had been answered.

Chapter Six

Preparations

Emily went home to help Ina at the farm over the summer months. She had wished she could go out on some summer mission, some endeavor that would fit in with preparing herself for her future work. But her father had requested that she spend the time with them, and she was anxious to honor his wishes where possible.

The summer eventually was over, though it seemed to Emily twice as long as normal. She was glad to pack her trunk and her suitcase and board the train for school.

But just maybe, she reasoned with herself as her train chugged south, *just maybe these weeks of canning beans and tomatoes with Ina were the very best way I could have spent the summer. Maybe even the best preparation. . . .*

Back into the rhythm of school life, she conscientiously obeyed the dorm rules, which meant that she was in bed on time. *I might as well be up studying,* she sometimes grumbled as she lay in bed with her eyes wide open, the threat of an impending exam hanging over her troubled head. Her grades slipped a little, but she struggled on, willing herself to make use of each precious moment of her day. *Lord, I trust you with my time, my health, and my grades,* she prayed.

Her social life dwindled down to almost none, and she soon became known as "Nose-In-A-Book Emily." She seldom had time to indulge in a leisurely stroll uptown or a game of table

49

tennis in the recreation room. But Emily didn't mind. She knew she needed to cram as much Bible learning into the short year as she possibly could.

She'd already had two interviews with the district superintendent, and on both occasions he had assured her that he would see she got a position as soon as she qualified.

A reading course had to be fulfilled, and Emily laboriously tried to fit it in along with her studies. It was difficult for her to read and report on all the required books, but if she didn't she would be delayed in getting a church posting. Her effort to keep pace left Emily hurried and exhausted.

Emily daily thanked God for strength, feeling that He truly was watching over her, certain He was as anxious for her to make it through the grueling school year as she was. Then two and a half weeks before the end of the term, she felt the familiar ache in her bones, the pinching tightness to her throat.

For a few hours she tried to deny that she had the flu, but her throbbing head and the flush of her face drew others' attention to her dilemma.

"Are you sick, dear?" Miss Herrington asked, touching a cold hand to Emily's forehead, and she had to nod in truthfulness.

"I think you should be in bed," responded the practical preceptress.

"I can't," moaned Emily. "I have a paper due tomorrow."

"I'm afraid the paper will have to wait," the preceptress continued. "Who is the teacher? I'll speak to him."

Emily told her and reluctantly headed for her room. By now the stairs were moving strangely. Emily clung to the bannister, scarcely knowing where to place her foot for the next step.

Miss Herrington came with some medication just as Emily pulled the covers up over her flannel nightgown and settled her head on the softly floating pillow.

Emily found it difficult to swallow as she tried to wash the pills down with a glass of orange juice.

"I will have Ruth double up with Judith tonight," the lady said. "That way you will not be disturbed and Ruth will have less chance of catching the bug."

Emily nodded.

"Do you feel sick to your stomach?" the preceptress asked.

Emily shook her head.

"Well, I'll leave this basin handy just in case," Miss Herrington went on. "And I will look in on you often."

Emily mumbled her thanks and willed the pills to work soon.

It was well that Miss Herrington had the foresight to leave the basin. Emily was soon in need of it—over and over again. *The medication won't have any chance to work,* Emily moaned. Miss Herrington was kept busy rinsing the basin and bathing Emily's flushed face.

For four days the chills and fever raged. Emily could feel the strength being sucked from her slight body. When she could think nearly coherently, she felt angry and disappointed that the day of graduation was drawing so near and she would not be ready. Her assignments were not completed. *If only—if only—* she argued; *if only the flu could have waited for a few more weeks!*

And then Emily had no more strength to fight. She gave in to the ravaging illness and was content to lay her weary, aching head upon the pillow and try to rest.

When she finally felt a little better, it was only a few days until the term would end. *I'm so far behind, I'll never catch up,* Emily concluded despondently. With reluctant and unsteady steps she made her way to the dean's office.

Professor Henry was more than considerate. He looked at all Emily's courses, promised to talk to the teachers, and assured her that they would do everything possible to help her to get the necessary work done the week she had left.

Concessions and shortcuts approved by the faculty along with Emily's hard work meant that she was somehow able to meet the requirements. But she had to lay aside her required reading. So when she finished the school term, graduating with her class, she was unable to present herself for service as a mission worker along with the others.

It pained Emily deeply when Ruth showed her certificate of approval and told excitedly where she would be serving.

"There is no church there—not yet. I am to start one," Ruth enthused. "I will have two Sunday services, actually. One in the Midland schoolhouse on Sunday mornings and the other at the Dunnagan school in the afternoon."

It sounded like a big undertaking to Emily. It also sounded wonderful. She gave Ruth a firm hug and wished her well, but tears flowed freely down both faces.

"Where will you live?" Emily asked when she had her emotions under control.

"I'll be boarding with a neighborhood family. I'm sure it will be crowded. They have a family of six, I've been told."

"Well, there's a good start to your church right there," Emily said with a wobbly smile, and Ruth answered with another hug.

But both girls knew that the situation would not be easy. Ruth had been raised as an only child and was not used to the noise and activity of a crowded house. And Ruth liked a lot of quiet time in which to think and pray and plan her sermons.

"I'll make it—somehow," Ruth said in response to Emily's look of concern.

Emily nodded, trying to coax up a confident smile.

"And what will you do?" asked Ruth seriously. "I know how much you wanted to be ready—now."

Emily nodded slowly, trying to mask the disappointment she was feeling.

"I'm going home," she said with just a small tremor in her voice. "I've been told I must regain my strength—and I still have to complete the reading course . . . so-o . . . ."

She shrugged and forced a smile.

"When do you think—?" began Ruth.

"Two or three weeks," Emily cut in. "I hope. Of course Rev. Witt has urged me to take a bit longer. Well, we'll see."

———

A few days later the two girls stood on the Regis station platform waiting for the train that would take Ruth to her first posting.

"Isn't it exciting about Verna?" Ruth asked enthusiastically.

Emily's eyes lit up. Verna Woods, another classmate, had

also responded to God's call to serve, even if it meant going alone.

"That will make three of us who are deaconesses," Emily said. "And we even get to go to conference—and vote."

Both girls laughed and gave each other an unrestrained hug. To sit on the conference bar was quite an honor.

The distant train wailed against the silence of the spring morning, and Ruth placed her luggage closer to the boarding dock.

"You'll write?" urged Emily.

"Of course. And you?" responded Ruth.

"Oh, I will. Promise. I'll have more time than you," Emily answered.

"Not if you are going to hurry through that book list," Ruth quipped, but Emily merely shrugged and nodded in reply. The reading course was demanding, and she knew her father would be carefully watching her to see that she didn't overdo.

There was just enough time before the train wheezed in for Emily to take Ruth's hand and bow for a quick prayer. Then the two friends parted—Ruth excitedly boarding the train to her first mission work, and Emily reluctantly returning to the dorm to wait for her train home.

More preparation, Lord? Emily prayed wistfully. But then she resolutely set her mind to the task at hand.

But rather than the two or three weeks Emily had anticipated, it was a full seven weeks before she had her books read, papers of approval, and was ready for her first assignment. By then her health was improved, her walk more steady, her face less strained.

Emily would not be boarding. A small living accommodation was available, she was informed by the superintendent in his letter assigning her to the small community of Wesson Creek. It was a two-day drive away from home by horse and buggy. Her father himself was providing her with a steady team of grays and a secondhand buggy.

Emily was relieved yet anxious about her assignment, for she had never lived alone before. She would be glad for the solitude, which would help her in studying and prayer time.

But at times it would be lonely, too, she reminded herself.

She felt thoroughly confused and strangely agitated as she saw her father reluctantly load the buggy for the trip, occasionally giving her long, questioning glances. She was both excited and fearful, exuberant and solemn, eager to be off and doubtful about leaving the home she had known and loved.

But she would not let the doubts and fears show. She kept the smile on her face, the spring in her step, and indicated that she was perfectly at ease with the path her life was taking.

Emily didn't know what all her father was piling into the already heavily loaded buggy. Gunny sack after gunny sack and box after box were stacked beneath the seat, spilling into the back of the democrat. She remembered that Ruth had set off to her assignment with just her two worn suitcases. *But Ruth is boarding,* she reminded herself. *I'll need to set up housekeeping on my own.*

At last the final trunk and small valise were settled into the packed buggy. "I do hope the weather holds," her father remarked with an eye on the cloudless sky. "Will Darin borrowed my only canvas tarp, and when I went over there this morning to collect it, his missus said he won't be home until next week."

Emily was totally unconcerned. With a sky as clear as the one that stretched above them, she was sure she could make a two-day trip without mishap.

Hugs and goodbyes were exchanged with her sisters and father, and Emily was off down the dusty road. A hand-drawn map from her father was tucked securely in her coat pocket.

The tears did not spill over until Emily was well hidden by the stands of poplar lining the country road. Then she allowed all the deep emotion to run down her cheeks and drip from her quivering chin.

This totally new venture—one she had been called to—was something she had to do, but it was not without some trepidation, some tearing away of old and dear bonds.

Emily made no effort to control her tears until she spotted a team approaching. She sniffed, took a handkerchief from her pocket, and hoped that she was successful in repairing the damage. A neighbor merely nodded and tipped his hat as they passed.

The sun was hot overhead, and Emily was glad her father had insisted she bring her everyday bonnet. She wore it now in place of the brand-new dark bonnet that was required to identify her as a church-approved deaconess. That treasured piece of headgear was protected from dust and sun in the small box at her feet.

Her father had picked a gentle team. Though Emily was by no means a horse-woman, she had often driven her father's well-disciplined team of bays. Shadow and Star, her new horses, needed little attention except to steer them in the right direction and urge them forward when they tried to loiter along the track.

Around noon Emily pulled the team into the shade of some larger poplar trees and climbed stiffly down from the buggy. Not used to driving a team for such a long period of time, she looked at her hands with dismay. Her fingers cramped and her hands felt as though blisters were forming. *So much for being a sturdy farm girl,* she thought wryly. She pulled off her bonnet and let the wind blow through her hair.

Emily unhooked the team and led them to water in the ditch. Shadow, eager for a drink, almost upended her in the dirty puddle. She spoke sharply to the horse and jerked on his bridle. Emily finally let go of the rein and stepped back to let him find his own way. She wasn't going to argue with the big gray.

After the team had satisfied their thirst, Emily tied them to posts where there was ample grazing, then lifted the bag with her lunch from the wagon. Ina had prepared it for her, and Emily's eyes misted as she looked at all the things Ina knew to be her favorites.

She was so filled with emotion that she could hardly swallow, so most of the lunch was rebundled and placed back in the buggy. Perhaps she would feel more like eating later.

The team was reluctant to give up the tall grasses. Emily had to drag on their reins and shout at the horses to get them back to the buggy. By the time she finally had them re-hitched, Emily was hot, sweaty, and angry.

At long last she was on her way again, the afternoon sun beating down upon her head.

"At least it's not raining," she muttered to herself as she flapped the reins over the two broad backs in front of her. The country road could be almost impassible when the heavy rains rutted the thick clay soil.

She was going to stay overnight with Fred and Agatha Russell, newly married and now in charge of the church at Conner. She was a little shy about seeing her former classmates for the first time as husband and wife. But as the afternoon wore on and the long shadows lengthened to darken the road she traveled, Emily no longer was concerned about fitting in at the home of newlyweds. She would be so thankful to see her friends and the parsonage that marked her abode for the night. She strained forward, eagerly scanning the road ahead for signs of civilization.

But it was almost dark before she finally spotted the small frame house. With a silent prayer of thanks, she turned the horses in at the gate. Her friends must have been watching for her and came out on the porch to greet her warmly. Fred took the team, and Agatha ushered Emily in to refresh herself at the kitchen basin before the evening meal was served.

Chapter Seven

Starting Out

Emily made her way down the path to the team that Fred had hooked to her loaded buggy. The sun was just making its way up into the summer sky. Emily knew it was going to be another hot day, and she firmly placed her bonnet on her head.

With warm thanks to Fred and Agatha, she settled herself on the buggy seat, picked up the reins and clucked to the team of grays. They responded with eagerness and Emily felt a twinge of guilt, sure that the horses expected to be on their way home. At the end of the lane, Emily had to force the team to make a right-hand rather than a left-hand turn. They reluctantly responded to her tug on the reins. She waved one last time at Agatha, and then Emily was alone once more.

Emily felt refreshed and eager after her night's rest. Her hands had been carefully washed and salved, and Agatha had even cut the feet from a pair of Fred's heavy discarded socks and snipped holes in the remaining portion for Emily's thumbs—a mitt of sorts to protect her from the wear of the reins. Emily wished she had thought of something like that before she left home.

The day grew hotter and hotter. Emily feared that even with the protection of her hat, she wouldn't be able to endure the heat much longer. A breeze stirred just in time.

As she had the day before, she stopped to eat, this time much past the noon hour. She had been watching for a place to water

57

her horses, but the ditches along the dusty road had been dry.

At last she spied a small pond. There were no sheltering trees nearby, but there was grass in the ditches. She guided her buggy off the road the best she could and climbed down. She was even more stiff than she had been the day before.

The horses, anxious to get to the water, were not too patient with Emily as she struggled with tugs and yokes. At last she separated the team from the buggy and led them carefully down the sharp incline to the edge of the water. The big mare was fairly cooperative, but Shadow, the gelding, lumbered forward and stepped on Emily's heel enough to cause her pain. When she squealed and jerked the rein, he threw his head angrily into the air, almost knocking the unsuspecting girl into the pond.

The two horses drank deeply, at length both turning their interest to the grasses at the water's edge. Emily tied each to a post and hobbled back up to the buggy to get the lunch Agatha had sent along. She was hungry. She was also thirsty. Even though the bottle of water Agatha had prepared was warm and uninviting, Emily drank nearly as long as the horses.

She removed her hat and pushed her hair back from her damp face to catch the full benefit of the afternoon breeze. Pulling her father's map from her coat, she saw she still had a long way to go.

She packed up the remains of her lunch and placed it where she could easily reach it if she grew hungry again before arriving at her own small parsonage. She eyed the horses as they greedily pulled mouthfuls of the coarse grasses. They hadn't been feeding very long, but, oh, she was anxious to be on her way. Her eyes went to the sky and to her dismay she saw large storm clouds boiling up in the west.

"Oh my!" she said aloud in alarm. "It looks like rain and here I sit right in the open! I don't even have a rain cape with me."

Rain was another thing Emily had not thought to prepare for.

She retrieved the team and hitched them hurriedly to the buggy while they switched angry tails and tossed defiant heads. But Emily paid no attention.

"We've got to hurry," she said firmly to the balky team. "It's going to rain and we are miles away from home." She smacked the reins on their round rumps, and they moodily started down the road at a brisk trot.

The trot did not last long. Emily knew the team was as tired as she, and she didn't have the heart to run them. They returned to a walk and Emily drove with one anxious eye on the sky.

The wind increased and Emily took another look at her map to be sure she was still on the right road. The impending storm didn't seem to threaten the horses in any way. They trudged along just as carelessly as they had done in the heavy heat.

But Emily was fearful enough for all of them. The dark, scudding clouds looked as if they would soak everything that was in the buggy. Emily cast furtive glances backward, trying to determine what was in each of the sacks and crates her father had packed.

She spotted bundles of sugar and flour. What use would they be to her if they got wet? She tried to think of some way to cover the supplies, but she could think of nothing. She began to pray, earnestly, fervently, for some divine intervention.

Just as the storm began to spatter angrily about Emily, she came around a bend and spotted a farmyard. Then for the first time she used the buggy whip, and the team started off at a brisk trot that Emily found difficult to control.

She did manage to direct the team into the yard, thankful that here was some help, but her relief was short-lived. The place was deserted. Tall grasses grew up around the buildings. Glass was missing from some of the windows of the aging house. Shingles flapped noisily in the tearing wind, and a large padlock held the door securely in place or it would have been flapping too. She knew immediately that no help would be found here.

She looked around and saw a sagging barn with a one-hinged double door and wondered if there was some way she could get the buggy in there and out of the storm.

It was hard work, but Emily at last managed to pull the huge door sufficiently open to fasten it back against the barn face. Then she tugged and pulled at its companion until she forced it open also.

She crawled back onto the now wet buggy seat and urged the team forward. There was just enough room to make it through the doorway. The horses were reluctant to enter the strange barn and snorted and sidestepped, but Emily would have none of their foolishness. She gave the gelding a sharp slap with the buggy whip, and his forward thrust encouraged the mare to follow.

Outside, the thunder rolled and crashed, and Emily prayed that the sagging barn would stay in one piece for the duration of the storm.

The horses restlessly complained about their unfamiliar surroundings. Emily decided she would unhitch the team and put them out to graze. The rain on their backs would bother the horses very little and they did need more grazing.

She struggled with Shadow and eventually unhooked him from the buggy. Star objected to her teammate leaving and tried to follow. Emily knew that she was going to have problems but spoke to the horse and hoped fervently that the mare would wait patiently until she returned for her.

The wind was whipping the heavy rain into lashing torrents now. Emily struggled against it to reach a fence where she could tie her horse securely. It would not do for Shadow to decide that now was a good time to head for home.

Against the wind and cold rain, Emily forced her way back into the gloom of the barn. Star had not been patient and, to Emily's dismay, had tramped around until she'd managed to break the buggy tongue. Emily nearly wept when she saw the damage. What would she ever do now?

She untangled the horse and led her, too, out into the beating rain. She found another post near to Shadow and tied the mare securely.

Back in the barn, soaked to the skin and ready to cry, Emily realized the first thing that she needed to do was to get out of her sopping clothes and into something warm and dry. The storm had dropped the temperature significantly, and her fingers felt like icicles. She rummaged in the semidarkness and found her valise and a fresh change of clothing. She drew back into the shadows, stripped the clinging wet garments from her shivering body and hurried into the dry clothing. Then she pulled the blanket from under the buggy seat and folded it about her. She needed all the warmth she could get.

Her eyes had adjusted to the darkness of the barn, and she spotted a welcome pile of dry straw in the corner. She made her way to it and tried to make herself comfortable.

Just when she thought she might have found some measure of comfort, rain began to drip from the roof above her head. Emily changed her position and went through the settling process again.

Then she noticed a small stream of water falling directly into her buggy, and Emily jumped up to make sure the sugar bag or flour sack was not immediately under it. The sugar was threatened, so she shifted the sack to a drier spot.

Back she went to her post on the straw pile again. A few new drips had begun since she vacated the spot, and Emily wondered if there was any place in the building where she was safe from the rain.

She hugged the blanket about her. There were more blankets in her trunk, but she hated to haul them out in the dirty old barn. She shivered and bundled herself more closely. She would just wait out the storm and then be on her way.

But the storm did not pass quickly, and Emily became more and more concerned. Occasionally she went to the door and listened for the horses. She could hear them stomping and chomping, quite content to feed while the storm raged about them.

Emily, too, was feeling the need for nourishment. She went to the buggy and found the rest of her lunch. She was glad she had left some of it for later. She wouldn't have known quite where to begin looking for a snack among the supplies in the wagon. Raw potatoes, ground flour, or bagged sugar did not have much appeal.

Emily ate the bit of lunch and still did not feel satisfied. If there were something to drink, she would feel much better. But the bottle of water had long since been exhausted.

Overhead the steady stream of pounding rain beat on the weathered roof.

"This is silly!" Emily said aloud. "All that water—and nothing to drink." She took Agatha's bottle and set it outside the door, hoping to collect enough rain to at least moisten her mouth and throat. Then she huddled down into the straw and tried to find some comfort from the cold.

She finally had to admit that the lack of daylight was no longer a result of the passing storm but because night was falling. Emily had never been brave in the dark. To be at home alone would have been one thing. To be in some old deserted barn was quite another. Emily was shivering now from far more than the chilly night air.

Again she went to the door and strained to look through the darkness to find the team. They were still there, feeding hungrily on the heavy grasses. Emily knew that she should remove the harnesses, but she could not bring herself to step out into the unknown blackness into the puddles and wet foliage.

With a shiver she realized that she was stranded for the night. Stranded with only moldy straw for a bed and no way to even lock the door against night prowlers. Emily had never spent a night in any kind of similar conditions before, and a knot of fear tightened her stomach. *My reading list surely didn't prepare me for this,* she thought wryly.

In the distance an owl hooted and Emily shivered again. In the corner something rustled in the straw and Emily had to stifle a scream as she scrambled to her feet. It was just a mouse, she was sure, but Emily was no more willing to share her habitation with a mouse than with a bear.

With what little twilight remained, Emily began to rummage in her trunk until she felt the warm, coarse fiber of a woolen blanket. *Dirt or no dirt, I've got to get warmer,* she told herself. She managed to tug it from the rest of her belongings and climbed up into the buggy. While pushing and shoving bags and boxes to make herself some kind of resting place, Emily came across a piece of heavy fabric folded neatly in a square. Opening it up, she discovered a rain cape her father had thoughtfully provided. *I should have paid more attention—I'm sure he told me about this,* Emily thought as she held the cape close to her heart and tried to swallow the lump in her throat. She wrapped up in the blankets as snugly as she could and spread the cape over herself as she settled in for the night. It was not comfortable, but at least it was dry—for the moment—and she hoped it would be reasonably free from other occupants.

Some time during the night the rain stopped. Then the wind died down, and from her cramped position in the buggy, Emily was able to hear the creaking of the harnesses and the tramping of the horses. The sound brought some small measure of comfort. At least she was not totally alone.

"Of course I'm not alone, Lord," she prayed. "Those were not just words I said to Papa—you really are here."

When Emily at last dropped off to sleep, her body ached, her throat felt dry from breathing straw mold, and her feet were cold in spite of her blanket, but the fear had left her. She knew in spite of her difficult situation that God was with her—just as He had promised to be.

Chapter Eight

Dubious Aid

A loud crack awakened Emily from her fitful sleep. She lurched up, surprising herself at her cramped position in the front of the buggy. For a moment she couldn't get her bearings, and then in a flash it all came back to her.

There was more commotion outside and Emily realized it was coming from where the horses were tethered.

She scrambled out of the buggy and ran to the door of the old barn. Shadow was causing the stir. He had exhausted the supply of grasses that he could reach on his short tether. In his greediness to feed on the rain-drenched grasses, he had managed to break the post and was now doing battle with a rickety fence. His halter rope still held him prisoner, for which Emily was thankful, but he had entangled himself in broken rails and rusty wire.

Emily ran forward, wondering how she was going to get the frantic horse and the broken fence free from each other.

"You think *you're* hungry," she scolded in frustration. "You've been feeding most of the night, but I've had nothing and—" But Shadow, still stomping and blowing, was in no mood to sympathize.

The horse needed to be quieted and the harness removed. Emily found this task most difficult, for the horse would not cooperate. At last she was able to pull the harness free and hang it on a portion of still-standing fence. Then she set to work trying to get the gelding to step through the broken rails and boards while she coaxed and urged him with tugs on the halter rope. He balked and snorted and dug in his hooves with each tug, finally backing up to the place where he had started.

Through the whole process Emily couldn't help but notice Star. She stood apart, head up, eyes alert and ears forward. Now and then she gave a quick snort as if to tell Shadow that life had played some cruel trick on him and she was in total sympathy.

Emily wished she could voice her own opinion about the circumstance. At last she did, speaking directly to the mare. "It's his own stupidity that got him where he is. I don't feel one bit sorry for him—and you needn't, either!"

"Oh, I don't. I don't," a male voice responded, and Emily whirled around, her face red with exertion. She had been so engrossed that she hadn't heard anyone approach.

The man who stood there was big and burly and roughly dressed. His beard—not trim and well kept but bushy—seemed to be there simply because the wearer felt it too bothersome to be rid of it. His clothing hung haphazardly on his oversized frame, and his trouser legs were tucked carelessly into the tops of his boots as protection against the wetness of the morning.

As Emily's eyes took in the appearance of her unexpected visitor, he leaned slightly to the side and spat on the ground.

"Whatcha doin' here?" he asked gruffly. Emily realized he had not moved an inch toward helping her.

"I'm—I'm trying to get my horse," she answered defensively, her eyes flashing as she spoke.

"Thet I can see," the man threw back, "but what's yer horse doin' on my property?"

His comment sobered Emily as she quickly surveyed the damage that Shadow had done and was still doing to the fence. At once she became contrite.

"I—I'm sorry," she began lamely. "I—certainly didn't mean to damage your—"

But he cut in sharply. "I never suspected ya set out to tear down my fence. But ya still ain't answered my question."

Emily's attention went back to Shadow, whose head was

jerking up and down against the rein. Emily didn't really blame him. He was standing in an awkward position, his legs sprawled over broken rail poles while two people who could help him continued to chatter. Emily tried once more to lead him to better ground.

Again he balked and snorted; then Emily felt herself being jostled to one side as the halter rope was grabbed out of her hand and the big man took charge.

Emily was glad to move out of the reach of both of them. She scrambled across the broken boards just as Shadow made a giant lunge and sent pieces of wood scattering as he headed for clear ground.

"Whoa-a," called the big man. Shadow obediently whoaed. Without a word to Emily he tossed the halter rope her way and began to throw the broken bits of board and poles back to where the fence had stood.

A flush washed over Emily's face.

"I am terribly sorry," she apologized. "I'll see to it that your fence is fixed."

Even as she said the words, she wondered just how she might do that. She had no money with which to purchase fencing materials, and no idea about how to make the repairs even if she had.

The big man straightened and looked sharply at Emily. Neither his voice nor his eyes softened. "An' how ya plannin' on doin' thet?"

Emily backed off another step and fidgeted with the rope in her hands.

"I—I don't know," she admitted. She'd made a mess of everything. "Perhaps—perhaps I can send for my father—"

"Jest like younguns," grumped the man, and he spat again. "Git theirselves in a fix an' yell fer their pa." He leaned over to grab another armload of broken fencing.

With nothing more to say, Emily led Shadow toward the barn. All she wanted to do was get away from those angry eyes as quickly as possible.

The man suddenly quit tossing broken rails. Emily, without turning to look, could feel his eyes on her retreating back.

"Jest a minute," he thundered; "we ain't done talkin' yet!"

Emily turned to face him, pulse racing, her face red.

"You still ain't explained what yer doin' here. You runnin' from home or somethin'?"

His words brought the fire back into Emily. Her head came up, her chin thrust out. "I am *not* a runaway child," she said with all the dignity she could muster. "I am the new deaconess for the area."

He stared at her in silence for a long minute, then blurted out, "The what?"

"The deaconess. I've been sent here by my church to start a mission work."

"Well, I never—" sputtered the man and he spat again.

Emily eyed him as calmly as she could, willing herself to get better control. After all, she was sent to the area to minister, not to enrage.

"An' who told yer church, whatever it is, thet we in this here area need to be 'missioned'?" asked the man, straightening to his full height until Emily felt as if she were looking at a giant.

Emily wasn't sure how her denomination had arrived at their decision to establish a mission in this community, so she held her tongue.

"Well—?" he thundered.

"Well, I'm not sure exactly," she began. "Perhaps—perhaps they were invited." She knew that was the case in many communities.

"*I* shore didn't invite 'em," the man declared, his eyes boring through Emily.

"No," she responded evenly, her eyes unwavering. "No, I'm sure you didn't."

They stood there, their gazes locked, some kind of challenge passing from one to the other. It was the big man who moved first.

"So how'd ya get here? I didn't see no wagon."

"No," replied Emily, shifting uneasily. "I have a buggy."

"Where?" The question was curt, short.

"In the—in the barn there." She motioned with her hand.

"So ya used my barn too?"

"I'm—I'm sorry. I thought the place was vacant. I didn't know anyone lived here. I—"

"The place *is* vacant. I don't need ta live here to own it, do I? It's bein' vacant gave ya license to walk right in and make yerself to home, did it?"

"No. Of course not. But when the storm struck—"

"Ya had to take shelter from thet storm? What's the matter? Ya made of sugar? Ya'd melt in a storm?"

"Of course not," answered Emily, trying hard to keep from responding angrily. "But I had supplies in the buggy that would have spoiled if they had gotten wet. I—"

"Supplies. An' ya didn't have 'em covered?"

Emily shook her head, feeling young and foolish all over again. She wouldn't bother explaining that her father had loaned his only canvas to a neighbor. The man would think her too young and irresponsible to care for herself, regardless.

He strode forward as if in a hurry to get the strange and troublesome interview over and the girl out of his yard and life.

"Well, let's git ya hitched up and outta here," he barked as he walked toward the barn.

"It's—it's not that simple," began Emily.

He stopped and looked at her.

"The wagon tongue—the horses—Star spooked in the storm and stepped on the tongue, and it's—it's broken," she finished lamely.

He just stared at her, open-mouthed and unbelieving. "You jest keep yerself an' those horses outta my way and outta trouble," he said tersely, and stalked off toward the sagging barn.

Emily's hand tightened on the lead rope and she jerked up the head of the feeding Shadow, tugging him toward the fence where Star still remained tied to a post.

"C'mon," she said to them in almost a whisper. "Let's not get into any more trouble," and she untied Star and led the team away from the fence, away from the barn, toward the lane.

Then she spotted the dilapidated Ford truck that stood at the entrance to the lane. For a moment her heart jumped, thinking another human was close by who might be able to rescue her from her present circumstance. And then she realized dismally that the truck likely belonged to the man who was fussing and swearing in the barn as he surveyed the broken tongue.

He was soon back outside, storming angrily as he headed for the truck at the road and rummaged in the back for some tools. When he walked back down the lane, he reminded Emily of last night's thunder storm.

Emily stayed out of his way all the while she heard the pounding and grumbling. When at last the commotion subsided, Emily debated whether she should approach the barn.

Fighting to keep the horses' heads up so they would not be grazing on any more grass that did not belong to them, Emily was hard put to hold them steady.

A gruff voice behind her said, "You can hook 'em up now." Emily just stared at him.

"You can hitch a team, can't ya?"

Emily's face began to flush and she fought for control of her emotions. She sighed, looked at the big man, and replied, "Yes. Yes, I can."

She gave a sharp tug on the ropes to get Shadow and Star going in the right direction. *But the buggy is still in the barn,* she thought.

Then even as the thought flitted through her mind, Emily saw that the buggy had been backed out of the barn and was standing on the grass, waiting for the approaching team.

She led the two horses into position before she realized that Shadow's harness was still hanging on the fence. With a red face she looked around, expecting to see the big man leering at her. But he was nowhere around, and then Emily heard the chug of the engine as he started his truck.

Emily led both horses around the barn so she could keep an eye on Star while she harnessed Shadow. Emily struggled as she made one attempt after another of getting the harness over the big horse's back. At last she got it on, and she sighed with relief. She was flushed and dirty and shaking from her exertion.

Maybe the girls who have to walk aren't so bad off, after all, she reasoned.

Emily led the team to the waiting buggy and hitched them for the remaining trip. She did hope that it wasn't far.

Noticing her dirty hands, a new thought came to Emily. She really was in quite a mess. Her hair was disheveled, her dress wrinkled and covered with dirty spots. She had planned to put on her deaconess bonnet just before she entered the town. Now, she reasoned shamefully, she would not wish to disgrace the hat.

"Oh, God," she prayed, "I've really made a mess of things. Could you show me a back way into town, Lord? I don't want to shame the church or you by coming in looking like this."

Emily clucked to the team and took her leave of the farmyard. It looked even more desolate and run-down in the light of day than it had in the darkness of the storm.

How could he make such a fuss about the broken fence? she asked herself. *Most of the fence is falling down.*

But even as Emily spoke the words to herself, she knew she had no right to wreck another's property—no matter what its seeming worth—without taking responsibility.

"I'll have to find some way to make things right," she said slowly. "But I've no idea how to go about it."

Emily remembered that she did not know who the man was that owned the property. Nor did she know how to get in contact with him.

"Oh, dear," she sighed, "that means he will have to contact me—and that makes it look like I'm trying to avoid my responsibilities. Oh, dear. I should have asked him—"

Emily turned the team onto the road and took another quick look at her map. But she wouldn't have needed to, for as she lifted her head she could see in the distance the small town where she was to serve. Her heart began to thud; then her mind quickly cautioned her emotions—both anxiety and excitement—to slow down.

"Surely the people won't all be like him," she voiced out loud. She reminded herself that though he was gruff and uncouth, he had rescued her horse from the fence, fixed the tongue of her buggy, and single-handedly pushed her buggy out of the barn. Even though he had been in a hurry to get her off his property, perhaps he really wasn't all bad and rude and uncouth.

Then another thought came to Emily, and it brought another flush to her cheek.

"I didn't even thank him," she said in a whisper. "What kind of deaconess am I?"

Chapter Nine

Beginnings

Emily could see no unobtrusive entry into the small town. As far as she could tell, there was only one road leading into it—right down the main street, between the houses and shops and the eyes of the townspeople.

Emily, her cheeks coloring, really did not wish to place the distinguishing bonnet upon her head. Nor did she wish to greet any of those who might be her new parishioners. But she did both. At the very edge of town, she reached for the carefully wrapped bonnet and lifted it out. With trembling hands she brushed her hair back from her warm face and attempted to push stray brown curls into proper place before settling the bonnet on her head. She brushed the dust from her skirts and tried vainly to brush away the wrinkles as well, and then clucked again to her team.

If she was going to minister to these people, she had to be friendly, she decided. So with that determination, Emily headed into the heart of town, ready to greet anyone she met with a warm smile and a nod of her head.

Though it damaged her pride, she kept her resolve, smiling and nodding to all she passed as though she were properly groomed and attired. She could feel their curiosity as she continued on down the street.

When she reached a large building called Wesson Creek Mercantile, Emily pulled the horses up before the building next

73

to it. According to her map, this was to be her home and the church for her parish.

It was not an impressive looking place. The paint had long since washed from the plain board sides. The door was sagging slightly, the two front windows dirty and broken, the walk in front of it covered with clutter. Emily looked at it in dismay. It couldn't be expected to draw people to worship.

For a moment she felt like crying, and then her sagging shoulders lifted and she forced a smile. It wasn't the building that mattered. She was here to share the Gospel. She would do that.

She tied the horses to the front rail, hoping that it was secure enough to hold them, and set off to survey her domain.

Through the gate that swung open on squeaking hinges, along the grass-hidden, broken walkway, toward the back where she understood her living quarters to be, Emily made her way.

The door would be secured with a padlock, Emily had been told, and so it was. But ironically, right beside the padlock, the key hung on a piece of rusty wire. Emily could not help but smile.

She opened the protesting door and entered the small closed-in porch. It was dusty, reeked with mustiness, and was full of spider webs. Emily ducked the webs and proceeded to the next room.

It too was small, with stained walls and a dirty floor. It held an old-fashioned wood stove and a small painted cupboard, with a wooden table and two chairs standing beneath the room's single window. In a corner a rough shelf supported a few discarded items. Two overstuffed chairs, ugly and defiant, sat right where they had been left.

"It sure isn't anything fancy," Emily breathed to herself, and then felt guilty about her evaluation.

"It's not that I expected it to be a palace, Lord," she apologized. "I just want neighborhood folks to feel welcome here."

Emily spotted a small door leading off the main room. The room behind it was not much bigger than a large-sized closet. A cot almost filled it. There were several nails sticking out of the wall boards, and Emily assumed they were meant for hanging garments on. No cupboard. No dresser of any kind. The bare window looked out into a weed-covered lot, and beyond was a weathered board fence.

Emily looked around her for a door to the part of the building that would function as the meeting room for church. There seemed to be none. She concluded that the only entry was from the outside and went around to take a look.

She knew the building had been used for a billiard room and assumed that it would be spacious.

The door was a little reluctant to open, but at length Emily was able to push it far enough to crowd her slight body inside. It took a moment for her eyes to adjust—and then she shuddered.

The room was truly a mess. The walls were dark and stained, the windowpanes shattered across the floor, broken chairs strewn here and there, and it looked as if the sparrows were in residence.

The floor was the worst. It was almost completely covered with litter, and where the wood did show through, it was stained and blotchy. Emily imagined that it had been used freely as a spittoon for as long as the building existed. With another shudder she fled outside. It was too much to deal with at the moment.

She closed the door tightly and hurried back to her little lodging. The two small rooms and the shed looked good in comparison to what was to be her church.

"Well," decided Emily, lifting her shoulders, "if I am to be settled by tonight, I'd best get busy." She went back to the street and began to laboriously unload her buggy.

Emily thought about conscripting some of the older children who gathered to watch her to help. After all, their backs were stronger than hers, she was sure. But she held herself in check and kept right on working in the afternoon sun while her little audience continued to grow.

Across the street, five or six youths lounged against the door of the blacksmith shop watching the goings-on with good humor. "Yeah, I heard rumors 'bout someone comin' to start a mission church," Emily overheard one of them say, "but I'd no idea that it'd be a *woman*—and she'd be nothin' more'n a young girl!" They jostled and teased and winked at one another, while Emily sweated under the weight of her loads.

Emily carried in all the boxes and bags of supplies and belongings, then the suitcase, and turned in dismay to the remaining trunk. How in the world would she get it off the buggy alone? Her father had had help from a neighbor to load it. She would just have to unload it item by item and leave the trunk itself on the buggy, or else she would have to drive the buggy away with the trunk and its contents still on board, with hopes of getting it unloaded later.

Deciding on the latter, Emily was turning from the buggy when a voice spoke from behind her.

"Need some help?" There was a hint of amusement in the tone.

Emily turned to see two young fellows standing near, their faces slightly red, their eyes twinkling.

The question caught Emily quite off guard, but a youngster who had been watching the proceedings with interest responded quickly, "She's got thet there big trunk. She cain't lift it."

"Want it in the house?" one fellow asked.

"Oh, if you could, please," Emily replied. "I would be so grateful."

One of the young men sprang easily up into the buggy and slid the trunk to the end where the other could reach one of the handles. With a bit of showing off, they hoisted the trunk and carried it down the broken walk to Emily's door.

"Where ya want it?" the talkative one asked, and Emily motioned to a corner of the room. The trunk was duly placed where she had indicated and the two were off, nudging and poking each other as they left with big, self-conscious grins on their boyish faces.

"Thank you! Thank you so much," Emily called after them and heard another nervous guffaw.

With the buggy finally empty, Emily took a deep breath and went back outside. She managed a smile in spite of her aching back and arms, her flushed face and disarrayed hair, and spoke as kindly as she knew how to the little group that still stood watching, "I'm Miss Emily Evans. I have been sent here to start a church. I do hope all of you will be able to be here on Sunday morning for Sunday school."

Some of the older boys, whom Emily judged to be ten to twelve, turned away quickly in seeming embarrassment. She had invited them to Sunday school—right along with the little kids.

Others looked at her blankly or nodded with shy smiles. Emily wondered how many of them had no idea what Sunday school was.

"We'll have singing and stories, and we'll learn about Jesus," Emily explained.

As the small group began to disperse, Emily untied the horses, picked up the reins and crawled wearily back into the buggy. Through the district superintendent, her father had arranged for the horses to be boarded at a small farm on the edge of town. Referring to her map again, Emily drove there now. It was not far to the farmstead, but Emily would have to walk back and she was anxious to begin her cleaning, so she urged the horses to a trot.

When she reached the farm, she noted that it really wasn't in much better condition than the one at which she had spent the night. A young lad met her when she turned her horses in at the gate. Emily was surprised to see that it was one of the fellows who had stood by and watched her unload.

"Hello," she greeted him. "I understand that my father has made arrangements for me to keep my horses here."

He nodded but made no comment.

"Would you like to show me where?" she asked him.

"Jest put the buggy over there," he said, with a motion of his head. "The horses can go to pasture."

Emily drove the buggy to the indicated place by the fence and climbed stiffly down. The kinks of the night before had still not left her body.

The boy stood and watched as she unhitched the team.

"What about the harness?" she asked him.

"Guess you can hang it in the barn," he answered casually.

Emily was about to move the team closer to the barn when a shrill voice came from the small house to her left. "Claude! Shame on you for making the lady do the work. You take those horses to the barn and unharness them. Then turn them to pasture. We're not paid for doing nothing, you know."

Emily turned to see a little bit of a woman standing on the porch. Over her small frame she wore an apron, startlingly white against the bleakness of the house. Her hair was pulled back into a severe knot at the back of her head, and from where Emily stood, the lady's face looked so tired that it seemed drained of emotions.

"Come on in," she nodded to Emily, "I'm Annie Travis. I'll fix some tea."

At the mention of tea, Emily's stomach reminded her painfully, sharply that she'd had nothing to eat since last night and it was well into the afternoon.

She wanted to decline the invitation and get back to cleaning, but her insides protested and so did her back. A cup of tea would be a good pickup. She managed a smile and moved forward.

"Tea would be nice," she admitted.

The contrast from outside to inside the little house surprised Emily. In spite of its simplicity, everything was spotless. Emily couldn't help but notice the small bouquet of summer flowers that graced the table and the clean shine of the cracked windows.

"Have a chair," Mrs. Travis invited and Emily accepted, worrying about her dusty dress on the clean wooden seat.

The woman bustled about her kitchen, pouring boiling water into a flowered teapot. Emily noticed a crack where the spout joined the pot.

"Sorry I don't have a cake or something," the woman apologized, then went on. "I do have some fresh bread—just out of the oven. You care for a piece or two of that with some strawberry jam?"

"It sounds wonderful," Emily responded and then checked her enthusiasm. She didn't want to sound as if she were starving. She blushed. "I—I always enjoy fresh bread," she added.

Mrs. Travis turned to cut the bread and get the jam from her cupboard. As she opened the door, Emily could see that the cupboard shelves were not crowded with provisions.

"So you're the new preacher?" Mrs. Travis said as she brought china cups from the cupboard and poured the tea. The cup that she handed Emily was without blemish, but the one she kept for herself had a large chip. She seated herself at the table and poured the tea.

"Well, I—I guess I don't really think of myself as a—a preacher," Emily fumbled. "More of a—a—teacher."

Mrs. Travis nodded. "Well, whatever you call it," she said, "we've sure been needing someone."

Emily's heart responded with a joyous flutter. *Here is someone with a welcome.*

"I was raised in church myself," explained the woman, "but my babies—haven't had a bit of church—any one of them." Her eyes darkened. "Sometimes I fear that it's too late for some of them. They've already been shaped to be what they're gonna be."

Emily was surprised to see tears form in Mrs. Travis's eyes, and she wondered if the mother was thinking of young Claude when she spoke.

"It's never too late for God," Emily said softly, and the woman's head came up, tears spilling slightly before she turned away.

A little girl entered the room and Mrs. Travis scooped her up onto her lap and broke a piece of bread for her. Then she brushed back the child's damp, curly hair and spoke softly, in a voice meant just for Emily.

"We don't have much. Used to be much better off, but my husband—he's—he's not been well—for some time now. Doesn't get things done like he used to. Things are getting—" But she did not go on. A haunted look flitted across her face as if she might already have said too much, and she abruptly broke off and lifted the cracked teapot.

"Care for another cup?" she asked and did not wait for Emily's answer before she began to pour.

Emily enjoyed a second helping of bread and would have

eaten a third and perhaps a fourth had not her good manners kept her in check. It would not do for her to be eating food that should be for the occupants of this needy home. So after her second slice of bread and her second cup of tea, she thanked her hostess, explained that she was most anxious to get her home scrubbed, invited the family to church, and excused herself.

At the gate she met another young boy—he, too, was a member of the little band that had watched her unpack. She smiled at him as she said "Hello," and he smiled shyly back. She noticed the thin, patched clothing, but she also saw a clean face and carefully combed hair. She decided that this boy also belonged in the simple farmhouse.

As Emily hurried back down the dusty road toward her own little dwelling, the picture of the small woman stayed in her mind. Here was someone in deep need. With very little means, she was endeavoring to care for a family—keeping the house clean, the clothing patched, the place a home, and doing it in spite of the fact that she had an ill husband. By the time Emily trudged down the crude main street, the warm summer sun beating down on her new black bonnet, her mind was already thinking of ways in which she could mobilize the community to aid the Travis family.

It's a shame, she thought, *just a shame that something hasn't been done.*

And then Emily felt a deep sense of joy. Annie Travis had wanted a church. A church for her growing family. Well, God had sent Emily in answer to that need. Emily vowed to do her best in ministering to this woman and her children.

Chapter Ten

Cleaning House

Pail in hand, Emily made her way to the backyard pump. It took a good deal of working the handle before a small stream of discolored water dribbled out of the pipe. She feared that her water supply might be unusable, but gradually the flow began to clear and soon clean-looking water filled Emily's bucket.

After returning to the house with the water, she carried in some wood for a fire. The thought of a stove burning in the little kitchen on such a warm day was not a welcome one, but Emily knew of no other way to get hot water for scrubbing. She was thankful for the good supply of wood that was stacked against the backyard fence.

After the fire was heating the tub of water Emily had placed on the stove, she turned to her suitcase for an older garment in which to do her cleaning.

"This dress is wrinkled and dirty," she said to herself, "but I don't want to ruin it entirely. I do need to change into something else. But where?"

Emily looked about her. The small windows of the kitchen-living room had no coverings. She looked into the bedroom. There was no curtain or shade on that window either.

"One of the first things I need are some kind of shades or curtains," Emily murmured, and then picked up her clothes and left the house for the small building out back.

The outhouse too was full of dust and spider webs. Emily

81

cringed as she entered. Dried leaves and grasses rustled beneath her feet.

"I do hope there are no living creatures in here," Emily muttered as she closed the door, then slipped her dress over her head and stripped off her good stockings.

Emily pulled on her old housekeeping dress as quickly as she could. She breathed a sigh of relief as she stepped back out into the sunlight.

By the time she had swept the two small rooms, she judged the water hot enough to begin her cleaning.

"Thank you, Lord, for soap and water," she breathed quietly as she picked up a cleaning brush and some soap, pushed up her sleeves and set to work on the bedroom. There wasn't much she could do about the skimpy, soiled mattress that flopped across the cot, but she could wash the walls, the windows and the floor. She would feel better about that.

When she turned to the kitchen-living quarters, she had to add more wood to the fire and more water to the tub.

By the time she had completed her scrubbing, dusk was falling. Then Emily remembered that she hadn't eaten supper yet.

She threw out the last of the dirty water, filled the basin afresh with warm water, and thoroughly washed her hands, arms and face. When she had finished, she turned with an aching back to her kitchen supplies. She was much too weary to spend a lot of time cooking, so she reached for a frying pan, scrambled a couple of eggs, and sliced some of Ina's bread.

She was about to sit down to eat her light meal when she noticed the kettle on the stove. In spite of the intense heat of the little room, she decided that another cup of tea would taste good. Then she settled at the table and bowed her head in prayer.

She was thankful—truly thankful. But as she raised her head the room before her made her tired shoulders sag. *Will this ever look like a home?* Even with her scrubbing, she had succeeded only in uncovering more blemishes on the walls, more cracks in the windows, more worn spots on the painted floor boards.

The dirt was gone, but her unpacked boxes and bags were stacked all about. Would her things fit in this tiny place? What could she do for cupboard space? The one tiny cupboard would hold very little besides her few dishes. Emily sighed. It was going to be very difficult.

But even as she looked with dismay at her surroundings, Emily thought, *At least I'm here—not off in a tumbled-down barn. It's clean, and there's no storm dripping water on me.*

Emily remembered the big, gruff man who had come to her rescue. She wondered again how she would contact him. She either had to fix his fence herself or pay for the damage that Shadow had done. She wasn't sure how she would accomplish either, yet it was very important that she not start off in this new community with a debt to one of the residents.

Emily sighed again. Perhaps someone who lingered around the blacksmith shop would know who he was. How could she describe him? There might be many big men in the area, and for her to ask if anyone knew a big, sour grouch with sloppy clothes and an unkept beard seemed hardly appropriate.

Emily sighed again. She would have to tread carefully. In the meantime she was weary and needed some sleep. She lifted her lamp from the small kitchen table and went to find blankets to make her bed.

———

The morning sun was already streaming in the open window when Emily awakened the next morning. For a moment she wished she had left it unwashed so the sunlight would not shine so brightly in her eyes. She wearily pulled herself from the cot, her sore muscles screaming their silent protest.

The thin, lumpy mattress had not allowed for a good night's sleep. The springs underneath sagged until her body nearly draped to the floor. She had not been able to properly turn over during the night. Emily stretched to loosen her cramped limbs.

She was running a brush through her long hair when she distinctly heard a woman's voice call loudly, "You boys get down off'n thet fence." The shout was followed by a thumping and scrambling, and Emily looked up just in time to see youngsters scrambling down off the fence that separated her yard from the mercantile next door.

"They were spying!" she whispered in horror. "The young rascals were spying on me." With a flaming face Emily whipped a blanket from her bed and hung it from nails on each side of the window. She looked down at herself, thankful that she still remained modestly attired in her "proper" cotton nightdress.

"I must get some blinds or curtains first thing," she announced to herself, hoping that something would be available at the mercantile next door.

And Emily hoped the prices would be reasonable. "I'm really going to have to watch my pennies," she went on. "It could be several weeks before the offerings are enough to support me."

After breakfast and devotions, Emily set to work trying to find a place for all her belongings. As simple as her requirements were, she still was hard-pressed to find room to store her things. It was afternoon before she had everything put away. Then she took a basin of water, her washcloth, and towel to her bedroom where, though she had little room, she was assured of privacy with the blanket over the window. After a quick sponge bath and a change into a clean dress, she tidied her hair, set her black bonnet in place, and took up her small handbag. It was time to do some shopping.

The few steps to the mercantile took only moments, and Emily pushed open the heavy door and stood quietly while her eyes adjusted to the darkness inside.

"Can I help ya?" a female voice asked, and Emily noticed someone behind the counter.

"Oh yes, please," she began, moving into the store. "I'm Miss Evans, the new mission worker. I—"

"I know who ya are," the woman interrupted, but there was no animosity in her voice even though it was curt and gruff.

Emily looked across the counter to the face of a tall plain woman. Her graying hair was pulled back tightly to form an odd kind of roll at the top of her head, her ample frame was shrouded in a cotton dress covered by a stiff dark apron, and her lined face looked as if it had long since forgotten how to smile.

But it was her eyes that drew Emily's attention. They were intense and piercing. Perhaps at one time they had danced with merriment or glowed with understanding.

"Oh . . . oh," Emily's voice faltered. Then she continued nervously. "I need some—some coverings for my windows. I have—"

"Yer right," said the woman briskly. "I chased them kids off the fence three times this mornin'.""

Emily flushed.

"Oh, it—it was you. I—heard a voice—I . . . Thank you," she finished lamely.

The woman just waved an arm and advanced toward a shelf at the rear of the store. "Jest curious—like kids always are." Then she went on. "Whatcha wantin'?" she asked.

"Well, I—I don't wish to spend too much. I would like curtains for the—the hominess, but I might have to settle for shades—if you have them."

"We do," the woman responded curtly. "Both. An' not too expensive either."

Emily was relieved. She followed the woman to the corner counter and waited for her to produce her merchandise.

Emily still felt as if she could not see clearly enough. She wasn't sure if the bolt of material the woman pushed toward her was blue or green.

"Could I—do you mind if I take it nearer the window?" asked Emily hesitantly. "I'm having trouble telling just what color—"

"Thet's John. He won't let us have the light on here in the daytime. Can scarcely see to get around. Says it's bright 'nough without it. Might be—if the place had some decent windows. Jest a waste of good money, he says. And besides, he says thet the light would jest heat the buildin' up more, and it's hot enough in here as it is in the summertime. Won't let no doors be open. Says the flies will come in—an' nobody wants flies in their molasses or pickles." She finished with a "humpf" and passed the bolt to Emily.

The material was green. Emily hated to say so, but she didn't like the color.

"Then we have these here blinds," the woman continued when Emily laid the bolt back on the counter top. "Not expensive. You could maybe make some light curtains to go with 'em for the same price as thet there heavier material."

Emily brightened. She looked at the light material. It had a soft ivory background and a small flower print, and Emily much preferred it to the rather sickly green.

Emily pulled out her measurement calculations. "How much would it be," she asked, "for the blinds and the curtain material?"

The woman did some quick figuring on a piece of paper and quoted Emily a price. It would cost more than she had hoped, but she did need to have some protection from curious eyes.

She nodded. "And I will need a spool of thread," she added. "I wasn't planning on sewing the curtains."

The woman added the spool to the list, and Emily drew out the required cash. It cut deeply into her meager finances, and she fidgeted as the woman cut the cloth and bundled her purchases. Emily was glad to escape the dark shop and head for home.

The remainder of her day was spent in putting up her blinds and hand sewing her curtains. In spite of the cost, when she was finally finished, she was pleased with the results.

But in some ways the clean, bright little curtains made the rest of the room look shabbier than ever. Emily sighed. She did wish that there was some way to cheer things up a bit.

———

The next morning Emily was back in the dark mercantile again.

"Do you have calcimine?" she asked the woman behind the counter, and the woman nodded her head and moved to a shelf behind her.

"Ya want tinted or white?"

Emily hadn't thought of getting tinted.

"White, I guess."

"How much ya need?" the clerk asked.

"Well, I—I don't really know," responded Emily, embarrassed. "I've never used it before—but the walls are in desperate need of some cleaning up, and I figured it would be the cheapest—"

"Yer right," the woman answered curtly. "Much cheaper'n paint."

Emily was relieved to hear that information.

"Ya doin' all the walls?"

"I would like to—in the living area. I haven't checked the—the church yet."

The woman nodded but said nothing. Emily wondered if she found it difficult to think of the former billiard room as a church.

"This ought to do if'n ya jest put on one coat," the woman said, lifting a can from the shelf. Then added, "Ya have a brush?"

Emily fumbled. She hadn't thought of a brush. "No-o," she stammered.

"Ya need a brush. No use buyin' one. You can use the one I used on the back shed."

"Thank you so much," Emily told the woman with a smile when a nice, clean brush was produced. "I do appreciate your lending it to me. And I'll make sure it comes back clean."

She paid the bill, mentally cringing as each coin left her hand, and then went home to tackle the job of whitewashing her little parsonage.

When the task was finally accomplished and the blinds and curtains were back in place, Emily looked around with contentment.

"Well, the calcimine didn't cover up all the problems, so it's not perfect, but it's much better—and it's clean," she declared. "Now I won't be embarrassed to have ladies in to tea."

Humming to herself, Emily set about washing up the borrowed brush. *Maybe she was going to feel at home here, after all.*

Chapter Eleven

The Church

Benches and a small pulpit would be arriving on the following Wednesday, thanks to arrangements by the district superintendent, so Emily wanted to have the meeting room cleaned up before then. The idea of a Sunday passing without a service distressed her, but there was really nothing she could do.

With a good deal of self-determination she gritted her teeth and picked up her broom and dustpan. The first task would be to remove the piles of debris from inside the church building. Then the scrubbing would begin.

Emily found an old apple crate, lined the bottom with a piece of cardboard so it would hold the clutter, and loaded it again and again as she swept the floor. Each time she filled it she had to carry it out and empty it at the back corner of the fence. She had quite a pile when the task was done—and the day was already spent. There would be no time for scrubbing this Friday.

Emily emptied her box one last time and dragged her tired body back to her living quarters. Her back and shoulders ached. Her face and hands were smudged with dirt. All she wanted was a chance to wash up, have some tea and a sandwich and fall into her bed—lumpy though it was.

It was early when Emily crawled from her bed the next morning and lit the fire so she could heat water for the scrubbing. During her work of the day before, Emily realized that some of the scattered chairs appeared to be fixable. There were also five or six crates scattered about the floor of the building. She was sure she would find a use for them. She had even found a back closet with shelves, which probably had been used as some type of billiard equipment room. It too was dirty, but Emily was thrilled at the discovery. It would be perfect for Sunday school supplies and hymnbooks.

As Emily entered the meeting room with her first pail of hot, soapy water, three sparrows made their exit through a broken window.

Emily set her pail on the stained floor and looked about her.

"I'd better fix the windows—somehow," she spoke quietly. "There's no use scrubbing if the birds are still living here."

Emily searched around until she found some scraps of board that she thought would do. She had discovered a few rusty nails on the shelf in the closet the previous day, and she went for them now. She was too short to reach the windows that needed repair, so she chose what she considered to be the safest chair to stand on. But she had no hammer.

Emily thought of crossing the street and asking the blacksmith to loan her one; instead, she went outside and searched her backyard until she found a rock large enough to use as a hammer. With that firmly in her hand, she began her repairs. It wasn't a good job, but as Emily studied the boarded-up window, she decided it should keep the birds out until a proper job could be done. Then she set to work with her water and scrub brush.

It was another long day for Emily. Twice she had to take rest breaks for her aching back and arms. At those times she found something lighter to do in the parsonage. She organized her books on the newly scrubbed small shelf and swept the rickety steps that led down into the cellar hole beneath the kitchen.

"I'm going to have to start cooking properly," she told herself as she sat down to another meal of tea and sliced bread. "If Father were here, he would say that I'll be making myself sick."

Emily quickly put the few dirty dishes in the pan on the

cupboard and hurried back to her scrubbing.

She didn't finish the task that day either. She groaned as she surveyed the small area she had managed to clean, wondering if she could possibly be ready by next Wednesday. Tomorrow was Sunday. There would be no scrubbing then. Emily felt a bit impatient that she could do nothing further till Monday, yet she was appreciative of a day of rest. She allowed herself the luxury of sleeping later and then arose to a leisurely breakfast and a long time of Bible study. She let the words from the Psalms and the Gospels rejuvenate her soul.

Then Emily prepared a nutritious dinner with vegetables from her father's garden and some of Ina's canned chicken, washed up the dishes that had been stacking higher and higher in the dishpan, and lay back down on her bed to read one of her favorite books. But the warm day outside beckoned to her. "I need to get out," she told herself. "A walk might help me settle down."

She debated about wearing her black bonnet and decided against it. *I'm not on church business,* she reasoned. *I'll just slip out down the alley and into the country.*

Walking felt good and Emily followed the road until she came to a little creek, crawled the fence, and followed the creek bank.

She loved the little stream, even though it seemed lazy and joyless, sometimes seeming to sit in disjointed, stagnant little pools.

She continued walking along the creek until she came to a spot where it truly did gurgle along. She sat down, her back against a tall poplar, and let the song of the stream ease some of the weariness from her mind and body.

"I must remember this spot," she murmured to herself. "It is restful here." She closed her eyes and listened to the song of the birds and the faraway bawl of a milk cow in the pasture beyond.

Just as she was close to dropping off to sleep there was a crashing through the undergrowth and Emily's eyes flew open.

Surely there aren't bears here! was her first frantic thought. But it was a man with a fishing pole who broke through the bushes.

Emily wasn't sure which one of them was the most surprised at seeing the other. He stared while she scrambled quickly to her feet, her eyes mirroring his surprise.

"I—I—was just resting," she stammered, and he seemed to gain some composure.

His smile was slow in coming, but when it did, Emily noticed that it was delightful. He nodded his head, let the smile come in full and then spoke slowly. "I'm not too used to finding a girl in my woods," he said with a chuckle. "Hello."

"But I'm not—not a girl," Emily quickly pointed out, making his eyes crinkle even more deeply at the corners.

"I—I mean, I'm Miss Emily Evans," Emily finished, as though that should be explanation enough.

"Miss Evans," returned the man with a nod.

Emily's face began to redden. She knew he still assumed her to be a young girl.

"I—I mean I'm the new deaconess. The mission worker sent here to start a new church."

For a moment the man's face showed surprise; then he smiled again. "Well, I should expect you won't have much trouble finding a willing congregation," he teased. "A pretty young girl—I mean, woman—" Then surprisingly his voice turned serious. "I guess your church knew well what it was doing."

Emily was at a loss to understand his words.

"What do you mean?" she asked softly, reading the irony in his voice.

He cast a quizzical glance her way. Emily's puzzled frown assured him that she truly didn't understand.

"People are always a bit more tolerant of girls," he replied. Then he cast a meaningful look her way and added, "Children—or defenseless young women."

By then Emily's face was flushed and her eyes flashing as she straightened to her fullest height and lifted her chin.

"I am not a girl," she repeated stubbornly. "Nor—nor am I a—a 'defenseless young woman.' I have been sent here to start a mission, not to—not to lure people to the church through pity. I—"

At the sound of his chuckle, she stopped and lifted her chin even higher. *He is insufferable!* she fumed. She would not stay and have him mock her further. With a defiant toss of her head she started back down the trail, but was quickly jerked up short. Her pinned hair had somehow become entangled in a branch.

Emily refused to cry out in spite of the sharp wrench. She lifted a trembling hand to disentangle herself. She could hear further laughter, and her anger increased.

In spite of her efforts, all she managed to do was dislodge the pins until her hair was tumbling about her shoulders. Still the small branch held her prisoner. She tugged and fumbled but could not free herself.

"If you don't spook, I'll help you," said a quiet voice from behind her.

Emily wanted to cry, but she choked back her anger, took a deep breath and willed herself to respond in a reasonable fashion. "If you would, please."

Never had she felt so humiliated. Never so at the mercy of another, particularly one so arrogant and irritating.

She heard him put down the rod he carried and step closer. Then she felt his hands on her hair. She sensed now that he was much taller than she and thus had an advantage—he could see what he was doing.

"Here's a—a peg," he said, thrusting a pin into her hand.

Emily almost corrected him, but she bit her tongue.

"Here's another," he said, and again passed her a hairpin.

"You *are* stuck!" he said as he began to untwine the locks of Emily's hair. In trying to free herself, she had managed to make things much worse.

At last he had untangled her hair and stepped back while she ran shaky hands over her hair to get it under some measure of control. She could hardly walk back to town with her hair flowing wildly about her shoulders.

"It's a shame you can't always leave it down," he surprised her by saying, and Emily looked at him evenly, making no comment in return.

His broad shoulders shrugged indifferently. "But I guess a mission worker couldn't do that."

Still Emily didn't answer. She feared he was taunting her again.

"Is this . . . your land?" Emily asked hesitantly, hoping to change the subject.

He shook his head. Emily was relieved that she hadn't trespassed a second time since coming to this community.

"It belongs to my uncle," he went on, and Emily's eyes expressed dismay.

He noticed, and another smile played at the corner of his mouth.

"It's okay," he assured her. "My uncle is a generous man. He'll share his creek with you. He even lets me call it mine."

It was Emily's turn to smile. He had understood her concerns so accurately.

"I don't even live here," the young man went on. "I've come to my uncle's farm every summer since I was a kid. I grew up in Edmonton. Live in Calgary now."

Emily hoped her face gave no hint of her confusion—he seemed so rude one minute and rather gentlemanly the next.

Her hair was secured as well as she could manage without brush or comb. Emily took a deep breath and made sure that no low overhanging branches obscured her path.

"Well, I must be going," she explained. "It'll be dark before I get back to town if I don't hurry."

"I have a car. I could drive you," he offered simply.

Emily blushed. What on earth would the town's folk say if she came driving into town with a complete stranger? She shook her head quickly. "No—no, thanks," she hastened to say. "But—I . . . thank you." She began to stumble down the path, anxious to get going.

"Good fishing," she called back over her shoulder in an effort to be neighborly. He waved a hand, and she heard another chuckle.

She dared not look back. He might still be standing there, watching her go. She really did need to hurry. It would be dark before she could cover the distance back to town. Then a new thought came, *I don't even know his name!*

Chapter Twelve

A Busy Week

On Monday morning Emily was anxious to get back to her scrubbing in the church, but she did take the time to wash three of the orange crates thoroughly and give them a coat of calcimine. They could be stacked as shelves in the corner of the bedroom, giving her some storage place. Emily could hardly wait for them to dry so she might place her clothing on the little shelves and hang one of her towels over the front.

Back in the church, Emily scrubbed all day Monday, all day Tuesday and Wednesday morning before she completed her task. Even so, she had been able to wash the walls only as high as her rickety chair would allow her to reach. The higher portion of the walls was not as dirty as the lower, except where the sparrows had been, but still the dust hung heavily on them. She had tried tying her cloth to the broom and scrubbing above her head with that. But it did a poor job at best, and finally Emily decided to leave them just as they were.

She was just throwing out her last pail of dirty water when the truck with the furnishings pulled in. Excitement filled her whole being, but as she watched the two gentlemen unload the benches, Emily's heart sank. The pews were very old and very used. Some church had replaced them and they obviously had been stored where the weather was able to get at them.

"They'll need a good scrubbing, too," Emily said to herself and looked down at her already rough, red hands.

The men were no more impressed with the little building than Emily had been.

"The windows need to be fixed," said the man named Herb Collins.

"The whole thing needs some paint," added Dick Lowe.

"I—I didn't have a ladder," Emily explained, pointing at the line on the walls.

Mr. Lowe nodded. "Must have been a dirty job," he said sympathetically.

"Is there a phone around?" asked Herb, and when Emily informed him there was one at the mercantile, he left the two of them and was gone for several minutes. When he came back he was carrying a ladder, which he put in the meeting room. Then he left again. Emily knew the men were no doubt hungry, so she excused herself to prepare a meal and went back to her little kitchen.

She was surprised when she returned to the church to call the men to dinner. Not only had the ladder been set up, but window glass, paint cans, brushes and various tools were all laid out. And the men had already set to work. Their first task was repairing the broken windows. Now Emily really felt excited. She would have some help in getting her church building in order.

The men decided to stay overnight to finish the repairs. Emily had no parishioners yet with whom to board them. She knew it would be senseless to offer her one small cot. The two ended up sleeping in the truck cab, assuming that the padded seat was somewhat softer than the church benches. Emily could only imagine how uncomfortable it must have been for them. She gave them her one spare blanket, then pulled the other one from her bed for them, too. She could do without the blanket far better than they.

The next day the men went from replacing the window glass to cleaning away the sign of birds, and then to the painting. Emily knew there was nothing much they could do about the splotches on the floor.

While the men painted the walls, Emily scrubbed down the wooden pews. But they were deeply stained and weathered, and washing wouldn't help that. She did wish she had some way to cover the discolored wood, but she was getting more help now than she had expected. She would not ask for more.

The men finished the painting just before the supper hour, moved in the pews that Emily had left drying in the sun and sat down for one last time to Emily's table. Then the truck disappeared down the dust-covered street and Emily was left waving at her gate that now swung on steady hinges. Mr. Lowe had somehow found the time to fix that as well.

Though dreadfully tired, Emily felt euphoric. It was only Thursday night. She had all day Friday and Saturday to make calls and invite the community people to the Sunday services. She could hardly wait to get started.

She lingered at the simple wooden pulpit after the two men had driven away, trying to envision what it would be like to face her congregation on Sunday morning. Her finger idly traced a large gouge that traveled over the pulpit's entire surface. It looked as if it had served for years in many missions as small as Wesson Creek.

But even the battered pulpit could not daunt Emily's buoyant spirits. It was not the building or the furnishings that mattered. It was the Word. The Bible was pure and righteous and unscathed by time or wear or even indifference. She could hardly wait for the opportunity to share it with this little community.

The next morning Emily bounded out of bed with the sunrise, eager to get started. *I'm doing much better at getting up in the morning than I did during Bible school days,* she thought wryly to herself. She spent extra time in her morning devotions—she needed God's help and wisdom as she went from door to door inviting people to the Sunday services. Then she groomed carefully and pinned her bonnet securely to her hair in case a breeze might come up. It would not do for the new mission worker to appear in public looking wind-blown and frazzled.

Emily set out, Bible in hand, with a brisk step. In her other hand was the borrowed paint brush to return to its owner. Besides, she knew no better place than the mercantile to begin her invitations.

Emily entered the store and paused to adjust her eyes as quickly as possible to the dim light. A figure stirred behind the far counter, and Emily hastened toward the spot, her voice preceding her with a merry, "Good morning. I am returning your brush. I can't thank you enough—"

But a gruff voice stopped her in her tracks. "My what?"

Emily instantly recognized the voice. It belonged to the man with the vacant farmhouse and the sagging barn. The man whose fence she had unwittingly dismantled.

"I'm—I'm sorry," she stammered, frozen where she stood. "I—I thought the store owner was here."

"He is!" the man snorted.

Emily's eyes had adjusted now. There he was, his huge frame towering over the counter, his face just as dark, just as challenging as she remembered it.

"I—I thought—" Emily stumbled.

Just then the woman who had helped Emily previously entered the shop. Relieved, Emily motioned in her direction, "I thought she—"

"Well, she don't," the man countered gruffly.

But the woman did not appear to be one bit intimidated by the size or the roar of the man. She approached Emily with an outstretched hand and accepted the brush from her.

"Did it work all right?" she asked amicably, to which Emily nodded dumbly.

"Did ya have enough calcimine?" the woman went on, and Emily nodded to that as well.

"My brother John owns the store," the clerk explained simply. "I keep his house and help out in the store a bit when he's not around."

Emily's eyes turned from the man to the woman. "I . . . I see," she managed.

"Ya had some help with the—the church," the woman went on, and the shine came back to Emily's eyes.

"Yes," she responded enthusiastically. "It's ready now—ready for Sunday. I—I dropped by to extend an invitation for service. Ten o'clock."

But the glow in Emily's eyes was not reflected in the eyes of the woman. "Reckon John and me don't feel much need for church," she answered firmly.

Emily had known she could expect refusals to her invitation, but now that she had one, she hardly knew what to do.

She quickly regained control, managed a wobbly smile, and said, "Well, should you ever change your mind, you'll be more than welcome."

Emily heard another snort from the tall man, but she did not turn to look at him. Instead, she addressed the woman, "And you are most welcome to come for tea—anytime."

She wasn't sure how to read the quick change in the woman's eyes, but the man scoffed, "Tea partyin' now!"

Emily turned to him then. She did hope her face showed a calmness she did not feel.

"I—I am glad to meet you again, Mr.—Mr. John. I didn't know where to find you, and I do still owe you for the damage done to your fence," she said.

"And thet ya do," the man asserted.

"I'm a little short of cash right now," Emily continued with flushed cheeks, "but if we could arrange for monthly payments—" She fumbled in her purse as she spoke and took out some coins as a token of good faith. She held them out to him, but the woman brushed her hand aside.

"Thet fence weren't worth a plugged nickel," she said firmly. "The rest of it is gonna fall down any day now."

The man cleared his throat awkwardly. "Vera's right," he admitted. "No need to make payment fer the fence." He turned abruptly and left the room through a door directly behind him.

Emily turned to the woman. "Thank you," she said sincerely, "but my horse really did damage his fence."

"I know. I know," replied the woman with a wave of her hand. "He told me 'bout it. But thet fence wouldn't have held nothin'—let alone a work horse. I have no qualms 'bout takin' money where money is due—but thet broken fence weren't worth nothin'."

Emily let the coins drop into her purse.

"And besides," the woman continued, "thet farmstead, old and out of shape as it is, it belongs to me jest as much as to him."

Emily murmured another thank you and left the store to continue her visiting.

Chapter Thirteen

Sunday

By the time night had fallen, Emily had visited nearly all of the homes in the little town. Though no one had been outright rude, Emily was wise enough to know that the various evasive answers she received to her invitation would likely not result in a high attendance come Sunday.

Still, there were a few homes where she had felt accepted and even warmly welcomed. At least some of the children appeared excited about the prospect of a Sunday school. Emily went to bed feeling that she had done her best, and promised herself that she would spend the next day traveling some of the outlying country roads.

But when Emily arose the next morning, it was to another thunderstorm and drenching rain. She knew it would be foolhardy to attempt taking the horses and buggy out in such weather. She settled in to prepare a Sunday school lesson and her sermon for the next day.

All day long the rain poured down. It was midafternoon before Emily thought of making some kind of signs to announce the meetings. At her kitchen table she wrote out the pertinent information on cardboard. Bundled up in a rain cape and galoshes, she started out, not quite sure where she could post her signs. One was tacked to the church door. She wished she could put one on the door of the mercantile. But with the poor impression she had already made on the owner, she dared not even suggest such a thing.

The blacksmith shop didn't seem appropriate for such notices, so she passed it by and went on to the drugstore next door. The man behind the counter seemed eager enough to welcome her until she explained her mission. Then his eyes grew distant and he fumbled for an explanation.

"Don't allow advertisin' here," he mumbled, but Emily knew differently. She had seen other local notices posted on his door and in his windows. He saw her eyes drift over the premises and hastened to add, "About religious things. Some folks are touchy about such things. I don't want to offend anyone, you understand?"

Emily understood all too well. She smiled brightly and left the store.

At her next stop, Sophie's Coffee Shop, Emily met with a warmer reception.

"Sure," said the plump, youngish matron called Sophie in a rather boisterous voice. "Stick it wherever ya want. This town needs all the excitement it can get."

Emily wasn't sure that her church service would be considered exciting, but she thankfully posted her little notice.

"Haven't had many folks in today," the woman commented. "Rainin' too hard. Why don't ya sit down and have a coffee," she continued. "Ya gonna make yerself sick, runnin' around in this weather."

How many times had Emily heard her father say those words? "I didn't bring my purse," she stammered, but the woman waved aside her comment.

"No matter. This one's on the house. Made this whole pot here, an' hardly anyone's been in. Hate to jest throw it out." Then Sophie paused and said apologetically, "Unless ya have beliefs against coffee drinkin'."

Emily smiled. She didn't care much for coffee, but she had no feelings about it being forbidden. "I would appreciate a cup. Thank you."

The woman took two cups from the shelf and filled them from the steaming pot, placed one in front of Emily and pulled up a chair to the table. "I'm Sophie," she said, pointing toward the sign on her door. "And you are. . . ?"

After Emily told her, she commented, "So yer startin' a church."

Emily nodded.

"I used to go to church when I was a kid," the woman continued. "My ma saw to thet."

"She sounds like a good mother," Emily replied with a smile.

But the woman quickly changed the topic of church. Emily wondered if she was a bit fearful of where it might lead.

"Whatcha think of our town?" Sophie asked.

Emily took a sip of the hot coffee. It did taste good and felt even better. In her short time in the pouring rain, she was already damp and chilled.

"I've been so busy trying to get things ready for Sunday that I've scarcely had time to form an opinion—but I'm sure I'm going to love it."

"You grow up in a small town or a city?" Sophie asked next.

"Neither," smiled Emily. "I was a farm kid."

"Me, too," the woman responded. "Hated it. Went off to the city when I was fourteen."

"Alone?" asked Emily before she could check herself.

The woman nodded her head and fidgeted with her cup, lifted it up and set it back down, then abruptly spoke to Emily again.

"Ya mind if I smoke?"

Emily was caught off guard. She did mind. The thought of a woman smoking—and in public—was, to her, shocking. She wondered if as the new mission worker she should express how she felt, but she looked at the nervous woman and said instead, "Go ahead, if you wish." Emily hated the smell of the smoke drifting around their heads, but she tried not to show it. After all, it was Sophie's cafe.

Sophie inhaled deeply, blew more smoke into the air above Emily's head and spoke again. "Didn't like the city, either. Tough place. Bunch of pushy people. I wasn't trained for any kind of good work. Cleaned rooms—tended bars. I hated it. Then I met Nick and we came here and got us this little cafe.

Well, things was goin' great 'til Nick decided this town was too
dead for 'im. He went back to the city an' I stayed on here."

She blew another cloud of smoke into the air. Emily felt that
she should respond, but she didn't know what to say.

The woman went on. "Heard later thet he got married again.
Well, I have the cafe. Not much, but it's a livin'. Me an' the kids
are makin' out fine."

Here was something Emily could respond to. "How many
ch—kids do you have?" she asked.

"Four. We had 'em one after the other. They was four, three,
two and one when Nick left me."

"I'm sorry," Emily whispered, picturing in her mind how
difficult it must have been.

Sophie grinned bravely. "So was I—at the time," she responded. "But now I figure as how Nick didn't do me so bad
after all. He really weren't all thet great a guy. Though he was
the best thet I seemed to be able to get. Now—life's really not
so bad. I enjoy the kids. Turned out pretty good, if I do say so."

"How old are they now?" asked Emily.

"Eight, seven, six and five," the woman answered, pride in
her eyes.

"I do hope they can come to Sunday school," Emily suggested
shyly.

Sophie puffed silently on her cigarette. After blowing a blue
cloud into the air, she smiled at Emily. "Sure. Why not?" she
agreed. "Didn't hurt me none."

On Sunday Emily awoke to the sound of more rain beating
methodically on her roof. Her first thought was of the Sunday
service. "No one will come in this weather," she moaned and
climbed reluctantly from her bed.

It was even worse than she feared when she looked outside
the window. The street was one large muddy pool. There was
not a soul in sight. Emily sighed deeply. She couldn't expect
anyone to brave such weather.

A morose Emily sat down to her breakfast. All her preparation had been in vain—at least for this Sunday. She wouldn't

be using the lessons today after all.

An hour before the appointed time for the service, Emily shrugged into her coat, wrapped her bonnet, Bible and lessons carefully in a towel and tucked them into a large pail, put the lid on and started the short walk around to the front of the building. She would be there, with a warming fire in the pot-belly stove, just in case someone did come.

Emily opened the front door to the church, pleased at least about the clean meeting room, but her happy expression turned to dismay. The roof leaked. Badly. Emily's scrubbed floor was now covered with dark puddles. A steady stream of rain water fell in a dozen places, the newly painted walls were streaked with trails of dirty water.

Emily was heartbroken. There were only a few benches in the room that were not rain-soaked. What would she do now? With a heavy heart she put down her pail and moved toward the stove.

The fire started slowly, and Emily wondered if the chimney was plugged, but suddenly the flames began to lick at the wood, and warmth spilled into the dismal room. Emily warmed her back at the fire and looked forlornly out the new windows while the minutes ticked by.

No one is coming, she finally conceded. *It is well past time. I might as well go back to the house.* She picked up her pail and started out the door, securing it carefully behind her.

The long day was not helped when the rain slackened in midafternoon—it was too late to aid her planned service any-way.

She went to bed early, hoping to sleep away the storm and her discouragement.

When she arose the next morning the rain had ceased, but the sky was still dark and glowering. Without hesitation she drew out her writing materials and began a letter to the district superintendent.

After a formal salutation and greeting, she got to the crux of the matter.

The church looked so nice, she wrote, *after Mr. Lowe and Mr. Collins kindly gave me so much aid in fixing the windows and painting the walls. But the recent rainstorm has brought to light the fact that the roof leaks badly.*

Is there any way that we could have some aid in fixing it?

I would normally expect the parishioners to care for such, but as yet we have no established church here. The nasty weather over the past weekend made it impossible to hold a service, so I do not even know who my parishioners are to be—or how long it might take to find them.

I would be most pleased if something could be done before the next heavy rainstorm. Of course, I know that funds are not in abundant supply, so I will await your good judgment.

May God grant you His peace and blessing.

Yours sincerely,

Miss Emily Evans.

After posting her letter, she took one more peek into the church building. Water still stood here and there, and Emily knew it would need to be sopped up before it could do further damage. She went again for her scrub pail and a heavy mop.

———

Emily's letter had more effect than she had dared to hope. Word came back by return mail that a crew would be there to repair the roof the following week—Lord willing—and might even have time to give the walls another coat of paint. Emily could scarcely believe it. *Thank you, Lord. You truly are here with me,* she prayed. With quickened resolve she decided to do more calling. As yet she had visited none of the outlying farms. She must remedy that before the next scheduled service. So bright and early the next morning, Emily determined, she would walk out to the Travis farm where her horses were kept, and begin her rural calling duties.

Chapter Fourteen

Visiting

Emily turned her team first toward the west. Consulting her map, she decided she would try to cover a seven-mile radius before the coming winter set in. She knew that it would keep her busy, but once she discovered where the prospective parishioners lived, she would concentrate her calls on those places.

There was no one home at the first farm. Disappointed, Emily drove the team on for another mile down the road to the next place. There she found a bachelor, and he made no bones about the fact that he wasn't interested in her little church service.

It was almost two miles to the next farm. Emily was pleased to see a woman at the clothesline, hanging out a washing that included a number of children's articles. Emily thought that home looked like a good prospect and turned the team in at the gate.

The woman stopped and lifted a hand to shield her eyes from the sun. Emily could imagine that the lady was studying the horses and buggy to determine which neighbor was calling.

By the time Emily pulled up to the hitching rail, two children had appeared from somewhere. A little girl clung to the mother's skirt, peeking shyly at Emily. The other, a boy of about eight, flopped a thatch of dark hair out of his eyes and studied her boldly.

"Hello," greeted Emily in her friendliest voice as she

107

stepped down from the buggy so that she might be on even ground with the woman.

"Lovely day, isn't it?" she continued.

The woman was hot and damp from bending over the sudsy water of the washtub. She blew a straying wisp of hair out of her face and looked up at the sizzling sun. Emily wondered if she had made a poor choice of words.

"You sellin' somethin'?" the woman asked candidly.

"Oh no. No," Emily quickly assured her.

"Come on in then," the woman invited, nodding toward the door with her head. Emily tied her horses and followed.

"Ed always says that the only people who call on us are peddlers—either of no-good products or unwanted religion."

Emily's breath caught in her throat.

"Sit down." The woman nodded toward a kitchen chair. The cat already had it occupied. Emily didn't know whether to shoo the cat off and take possession or remain standing. The little girl solved the problem. She stepped forward and smacked the cat off with a pudgy hand. Emily took the seat.

"You new here?" the woman asked while she pushed the teakettle forward and poked another stick into the fireplace.

"Yes—yes, I am," Emily answered rather breathlessly. She wasn't quite sure how to handle the situation. "I've been here only a couple of weeks, in fact." There was heavy silence. "I— I decided that I should get out and meet my neighbors," Emily continued. Well, it was the truth as far as it went, she told herself. "My name is Emily," she added.

"I'm Clara. Who's farm you on?" asked the woman.

"Oh, I'm not on a farm," Emily admitted reluctantly.

Clara frowned as she lifted down the teapot. "In town?" she asked doubtfully.

"Yes. In town," responded Emily with her best smile.

"Well—I never," the woman said.

"Pardon me?"

The woman turned to look at Emily. She was shaking her head. "Never a town woman called to make acquaintance before," she observed dryly.

Emily felt as if she were living a lie. She knew she must

clear up the matter quickly or she would not be able to live with herself. Her face reddened as she stood to her feet.

"Actually," she said slowly, "I am the new—new mission worker in town. My church hopes to start a congregation here. I—I am just trying to get acquainted so that I may find out who—who would be interested in joining us."

Clara had set down the teapot. She stood with mouth open, staring at Emily.

"Just like Ed says." The farmwife spoke quietly, a look of disappointment in her eyes.

"You aren't interested in church?" Emily asked shyly.

The woman turned her back and put the pot back up on the shelf.

Emily did not wait for her answer. "Then, perhaps—perhaps I could call—just as a friend. We wouldn't talk church at all— just visit."

The woman said nothing, but Emily noticed that she was taking the teapot down again.

Emily held her tongue for the moment, thinking quickly. She must try hard not to say anything that might jeopardize the delicate opportunity.

"I noticed that you have some lovely flowers, Clara," she ventured and the woman's eyes lit up for the first time.

"I'm not familiar with that blue one at the corner of the house," Emily went on.

"Got those seeds from my mother," said Clara. "She always had a patch of 'em. Called Blue Cups."

"They are beautiful," continued Emily sincerely.

"You can have a few seeds come fall—if you'd like," offered Clara, then added slowly, "That is, if you're plannin' to stay over the winter."

"Oh, I am," Emily spoke hurriedly. "I hope I can stay for a long time."

Clara smiled slightly.

They had their tea together and chatted about flowers, family and housekeeping. Emily did not bring up the subject of church again. Nor did her companion. Emily sensed that Clara was starved for the fellowship of another woman. Although

Emily hated to leave, the sun was climbing directly up overhead and she knew she should be on her way. Besides, she was afraid that Ed might suddenly make an appearance, and she was not sure she was prepared as yet to meet the man, who would immediately assume she was a peddler.

When at last she bid farewell, Clara was reluctant to let her go. Then Emily turned her team and called back as she drove off, "You must have tea with me when you're in town. I live at the back of the old pool hall," deciding it was wiser in this case to identify her residence by what the building had been.

"Well, I certainly haven't added many members to my congregation this morning," Emily mused as she turned her horses onto the road and set off for the next farm.

This one belonged to the Browns, Emily learned when she was cordially greeted, though not asked to come in. Mrs. Brown listened to her invitation, thanked her for her kindness and said she would consider letting her children attend. Emily was afraid she would not see them in her little church. She lifted her heart in prayer for the Brown family.

By the time Emily had taken to the road once again, she discovered she was hungry and decided to break for the light lunch she had tucked beneath the buggy seat.

"Most people will invite the visiting preacher in for a meal if it is anywhere near mealtime," Rev. Witt had told the students during a school chapel service. "But one is wise not to count on it. Take a bit of a lunch with you if you are expecting your calls to take most of your day" he advised.

As soon as she felt the team had fed long enough, she arose from the grassy shade, stretched, and climbed back up in her buggy.

There were still some bad potholes in the low spots from the last heavy rain, and Emily drove carefully. She had no desire to get mired down while dressed in her best Sunday frock and shoes.

She seemed to drive endlessly before the next farmyard came into view. Emily turned in at the gate and was met by a fiercely barking farm dog. The horses were reluctant to enter the yard and began backing their way toward the gate again.

Emily had a hard time keeping the team under control. She knew there was no way she was going to climb down from the buggy until the dog's owner made an appearance.

But though Emily saw the curtain at the window moving as if some hand were sweeping it aside, no one appeared at the door. Emily finally managed to get her team turned around and back to the road.

It was late by then and Emily wearily decided to head for home. It was a long drive back to town and she wanted to make it over the potholes while there was still plenty of light.

It was close to the supper hour when Emily again passed the farm she had visited that morning but found no one home. Now a small truck stood in the yard and a man carrying a pail crossed toward the barn. Emily could see a woman in a printed housedress coming from the chicken pens, a basket in her hand.

Impulsively, Emily turned her horses in at the gate. She would make a quick call while she was passing. She couldn't do any worse than she had already done.

At the sound of the approaching buggy, the woman stopped and turned to watch it draw near. A light breeze toyed with the strings of the woman's apron and lifted wisps of graying hair. There was a slight smile of greeting on her pleasant, motherly face. Emily felt it was the most welcome sight she had seen all day, and responded with a bright smile.

"Hello," called the woman before Emily had even stopped the team. Emily returned the greeting.

The woman did not wait for Emily to alight, but as soon as the horses arrived at the hitching rail, she set down her basket of fresh eggs and moved forward to tie the team herself.

"You out calling?" the woman asked.

"That's right," Emily answered, surprised that she would know. Emily brushed the wrinkles from her skirt, trying at the same time to shake some of the kinks from her back and legs as she stepped down from the buggy.

"I'll just stop a minute," Emily said. "I know it is an awkward hour, but you weren't home when I passed by this morning."

"You've been calling all day?" the woman asked, then

quickly continued, "My, you must be exhausted."

Emily just smiled.

"Come in," invited the woman, picking up her basket again and shooing away a kitten that rubbed against her leg.

"Oh, but I mustn't stop now," Emily answered. "It is almost the supper hour."

"So join us," she replied pleasantly. "It won't be fancy, but we fare quite well—and we love company. There's just George and me. Come on."

Emily gratefully followed her into the restful coolness of the farmhouse.

"I take it you are the new church worker." The woman again surprised Emily. She added, "But I don't know your name."

"It's Emily. Emily Evans."

"I'm Molly Reilly. I heard you were in town. My, what a job you have—making that old hall into a church," she chuckled lightly.

Emily nodded. "I thought I had it pretty well in hand," she admitted, "until that heavy rain over the weekend."

"It leaks?" the woman asked sympathetically.

"It leaks," agreed Emily. "Badly."

"Oh, dear!" exclaimed Mrs. Reilly kindly. "What a shame."

Emily liked her immediately; perhaps drawn toward the woman because of the mother Emily had lost. She was glad she had decided to stop.

"Take off your hat and lay it on the shelf there," her hostess invited. "The washbasin is right over there and there's no shortage of water."

Emily moved to comply.

"I believe you met our nephew," the woman said off-handedly as Emily freshened up at the basin. Emily wondered if their nephew was one of the young lads who had carried in her trunk.

"Shad Austin," the lady explained further.

Emily still drew a blank. She shook her head slowly.

"He came back from fishing and said you had met along the creek."

Emily could feel her face burning. What else might the

young man have told about her?

"He thought you looked awfully young to be taking on so much responsibility," the woman added comfortably as she bustled about her big farm kitchen.

I'll bet he did, Emily wanted to retort, but she bit her tongue.

"Shad's father was a preacher," the woman explained, surprising Emily beyond measure. From the young man's response to her "calling," she hadn't expected him to have had Christian rearing.

"At one time Shad planned on being a preacher, too, but that was before—" Mrs. Reilly sighed and her shoulders sagged, and she said no more.

Emily pondered what it all meant. At one time? Before what? What had happened? She wanted to know but of course didn't feel free to ask.

"He's a banker now," his aunt continued. "In Calgary. He still comes to the farm whenever he can. His folks are both gone now, and he's always been like a son to George and me."

Then she chuckled. "He came home last Sunday and said, 'Aunt Moll'—he always calls me Aunt Moll—'guess what I just found along the creek. A new preacher. A little bit of a girl. Going to start services in town. Maybe you'd better check her out, Aunt Moll. See if she's teaching the truth.' "

Emily's face flushed deeply. She winced at the thought of being "checked out." Certainly she planned to teach the truth. It was unkind of the young man to suggest she might do otherwise.

"Well, George gave me a wink, but Shad seemed quiet— almost moody—for the rest of the day. And he's never like that. After we'd gone to bed, George and I had a long talk. Wouldn't it be something if our Shad made his way back to God? It would sure be an answer to his mother's prayers—and ours." She sniffed and turned back to Emily, wiping her eyes.

"Forgive me," she implored. "It's just that we've been praying for him for so long. We grasp at any signs of softening toward the Lord, I guess."

Emily managed a smile and whispered a quiet, though sincere, "I'm so sorry." Mrs. Reilly returned the smile and went back to her stove.

"George will be looking for his supper," she said as she worked. "He's only milking two cows now and it doesn't take him long."

"Is there anything I can do?" offered Emily, certain now that she was staying for supper.

"You can set the table," Mrs. Reilly invited. "You'll find the dishes in that cupboard right there."

Chapter Fifteen

Another Week

Emily's calling continued to be met with varied responses. Very few folks gave her a definite answer, but there were some who said they would consider coming to her little church, or would think about sending their children. Emily found their indecision frustrating, but she had to accept it and keep praying for these families. Those long buggy rides between farms were good times for that, she discovered.

"The weather can't be an excuse *this* time," Emily mused as she looked out on a perfect Sunday morning.

Singing to herself, she prepared for the service. Surely today would be very different from last week.

At two minutes to ten, Mrs. Travis and two of her children found their way into one of the pews. Emily smiled her good morning, hopeful that they were only the first of many.

They waited for another fifteen minutes, but no one else came. So Emily, with a heavy heart, started the Sunday school lesson. Maybe others would join them later for the morning service, but she was disappointed in that as well.

Don't despair, she kept telling herself. *This is only the beginning. And perhaps God wants me to spend special, personal time with this woman and her children.* Emily endeavored to make Mrs. Travis and her two little ones feel as much in the presence of the Father as she knew how.

When the short Bible lesson and the worship service had

ended, the woman took Emily's hand and smiled her appreciation.

"It is good to be in church again," she said in a soft voice. "I have missed it so much. Especially since Mr. Travis is—is ill."

"I'm so glad you could come," Emily responded, and then impulsively gave the older woman a warm hug.

The woman left with tears in her eyes, and Emily lingered about the room, straightening the few worn hymnals and studying the stains on the walls.

Her first Sunday had not been as she would have chosen. But certainly God cared even more about this community and these people than she did. He would help her get their attention.

On Tuesday a work crew of six men in two trucks pulled up in front of Emily's little church. She was both excited and concerned when she saw the number of men. She would be expected to feed them. Emily knew her cupboards didn't hold much in food staples.

She smiled her welcome, reminding herself that she had written the letter asking for help. God had answered her need. And, surely, if He had supplied the men and the materials, He would supply their food as well.

And He did—through Shad's Aunt Moll. Mrs. Reilly was shopping at the mercantile when the trucks pulled in and the men busied themselves setting up their ladders. Quick to assess the situation, she hastened to Emily's door and rapped hurriedly.

Emily answered, still a bit flustered by the situation.

"I see you have a whole crew out here," said Mrs. Reilly.

"Yes," responded Emily.

"And I suppose you're expected to feed them?" asked the woman.

Emily nodded, her face showing her concern.

"I guessed as much," the woman went on. With a hint of apology she lowered her voice, "Can you cook?"

Emily nodded and smiled.

"Good!" said the older woman. "So many of the younger generation . . ." But she stopped and changed direction, "Well, you fix something for their noon meal, soup and bread—or whatever you have—and I'll fry a couple chickens and make some pies for their supper."

Emily couldn't believe her ears. "Oh-h, but—" she began, but the woman stopped her with a wave of her hand.

"You have vegetables?"

Emily thought of the garden produce her father had sent along. She nodded.

"Then you take care of that. I'll see to the other."

And she was off before Emily could even find the words to express her relief and gratitude.

As Emily watched Molly Reilly hasten down the broken walk, a thought flashed through her mind. *I wonder where you were on Sunday?* but she quickly checked herself. That was none of her business. She was not sent to judge the people—only to present truth and lead them to the Lord.

Emily was just about to reenter her little home when she saw Sophie waving a tea towel from down the street. "Yoo-hoo" came the call. Emily hastened across the dusty road, hoping nothing was wrong at Sophie's place.

"Is—is anything the matter?" she exclaimed when she was within earshot.

Sophie laughed with unchecked hilarity. "No. No. Nothin' like thet. Jest saw yer big crew and figured ya might not have a coffeepot big enough to serve 'em all. Why don't ya send 'em all over here at coffee time? I'll supply the coffee—you send the men."

Emily stared open-mouthed. She hadn't even thought about coffee time.

She nodded her agreement, thanked Sophie and asked what time she would like the crew to come.

"Tenish," the woman responded. Emily scurried back to the house to get some cookies in the oven. At least she could supply that much to go with the coffee.

———

At ten the crew was called from their labors and sent over to Sophie's cafe for morning coffee and cookies. At noon, Emily served thick vegetable soup and sliced bread. In the afternoon, Sophie again served coffee, and Emily had time to bake a chocolate cake. And, right on time for the supper hour, Reillys' truck pulled up in front of the building and Mrs. Reilly came in bearing her dishes of fried chicken and apple pies.

When the long day had come to a close, the roof was repaired and the walls repainted. One older man had even found time to replace the broken boards in Emily's walk, while a younger member of the crew worked a scythe in her backyard, taking down all the tall grass and garden weed patch. Emily couldn't believe how much had been accomplished in such a short time.

Deeply thankful, Emily lay on her bed that night. The little church and her small abode were now in good order. She could concentrate her efforts on reaching out with love and truth to the people of the community.

Emily's days were mostly taken up with her calling. At times she came home weary and disappointed. There just didn't seem to be much interest in her little mission church. With difficulty she left her burden with the Lord and tried to sleep in spite of her anxiety.

A letter from Ruth was filled with excitement and good news. She loved her community, she loved her boarding place, and she had crowded twenty-five people into one little country schoolhouse on her first Sunday of preaching—twenty-nine in the other and the numbers had continued to grow. Now the attendance had settled in at thirty to forty at each service.

Ruth is such a good preacher that they are sure to come to hear her, thought Emily, holding the pages loosely and staring out at the vacant lot. She was happy for Ruth—but in comparison, Emily did seem to be a total failure.

She went to bed feeling discouraged and lay tossing restlessly. Finally she crawled out and knelt down on the braided rug by her beside.

"Lord," she prayed, "I was sure I heard your call to serve. I don't seem to be very good at it. I can't preach like Ruth. I know that. Maybe I misunderstood the feeling I had in chapel. I don't know, God. I'm so mixed up." Emily paused a moment to think. "But that strong desire to serve you in some way was there even before I went to Bible school. Surely that was from you, Lord." She paused again. "If you really want me to start this little church, then I need your help. I can't do it without you. Please, dear God—give me wisdom and direction.

"I'm willing to work here—for as long as it takes—if that is your will. Show me, Lord. Show me what to do.

"And help me to be patient. I know I'm always in a hurry. I know I push. I've always pushed myself, Lord. I'm not good at learning things and I've had to work harder at it than others.

"But help me to not push other people and to understand that this is your work, not mine. I don't need to push here. I need to obey. And I need to wait for you."

Emily continued praying, the tears wetting her cheeks. At length she felt a peace steal over her heart and she rose from her knees, brushed her tear-stained face with a sleeve of her nightgown and climbed back into bed.

She slept then. A restful, much-needed sleep.

Whatever happened at Wesson Creek Mission was up to the Lord. Emily was only an instrument for Him to use.

———

The next morning Emily arose with better spirits. It was Sunday and she expected to again welcome Mrs. Travis and her children to the service, intending to use the time together as well as she was able. But when the Travis children arrived at the door of the little church, they were alone.

"Mama's not well," they informed Emily in quiet voices and selected the same seat they had occupied the previous Sunday.

Emily was about to begin the lesson when the door opened again and Mrs. Reilly scurried in, her face red, her hat slightly akimbo. But she flashed a smile at Emily.

"The cows got out. Just when we were ready to leave. George is still rounding up the last of them. Neither of us would have made it to church if we'd had to drive all the way to Tomis like we've been doing. It's nice to have our own church here in town."

She slid into the seat beside the Travis children, still panting slightly. "Don't know why such things always happen on Sunday," she puffed, drawing a white handkerchief over her perspiring face.

Emily smiled, welcomed her little audience and began her lesson.

She had just announced the story of Noah and the ark when the door opened again and Sophie stuck her head in. "Sorry," she said in a hoarse whisper. "They was scared to come alone the first time." She pushed four children with shiny-clean faces and slicked-down hair into the room, withdrew and closed the door again.

Emily, happy indeed for a congregation of seven, greeted the four newcomers.

When it was time for the morning worship service, three more people joined them—two country women, one leading her child by the hand.

That's ten! thrilled Emily, but she did not pause long to rejoice. It was not her doing. God had sent them to her. Now it was her responsibility to teach from His Word.

As soon as Emily had eaten her simple dinner, she placed some cookies and a loaf of bread in a pail and set out for the Travises. She knew there wasn't much she could do about the illness itself, but at least she would express her concern and see if there was any way that she could help.

She expected to find the woman in bed, or at least in the house wrapped in blankets and drinking broth. But when Emily arrived Mrs. Travis was in her garden, pulling carrots. She straightened and her hand fluttered to her face. She looked surprised at Emily's visit, and Emily knew she had caught her off guard.

Emily almost blurted out, "The children said you were not feeling well," but said instead, "I brought some cookies. Thought we could have tea. How are you? I—I missed you at the service."

Emily noticed that the woman turned sideways when she answered.

"That's—that's kind. Come in. I—I wasn't feeling so well this morning. Better now." And she led the way to the house.

It wasn't until they were seated at the kitchen table having tea and cookies that Emily noticed a large discolored area on the left side of the woman's face. Mrs. Travis seemed to sense immediately that Emily had seen the bruise.

"I fell," she offered quickly. "It's nothing."

"But it looks . . . shouldn't you see a doctor?"

Mrs. Travis shook her head stubbornly. "No need," she insisted.

"Did you faint?" asked Emily. Perhaps the woman was sicker than she realized. But Mrs. Travis brushed aside the question.

"No. No. Don't think so. Just—just clumsy, I guess."

Emily let the matter drop. She could sense that the woman was agitated.

While Emily was on her way home, she tried to puzzle through the situation. *Perhaps she has seizures and doesn't want to admit it,* she reasoned. *But there must be some kind of medication that could help her. But, then, maybe not . . .*

Maybe Mrs. Travis would not visit the doctor because of lack of funds. Or she might just refuse to admit the seriousness of her illness because of the children. Mr. Travis was hardly able to care for them with his own ill health.

Whatever the situation, the Travises needed her support and her prayers. She hoped that other members of the community were aware of their circumstances and ready to help as well.

After another busy week of calling in all kinds of weather—hot one day and a cold rain the next—Emily awakened early on Friday. She lay in her bed staring up at the ceiling while it seemed to sway and tilt every which way. She felt flushed, her throat hurt and her body ached.

"Oh no!" she groaned. "I can't be sick. Lord, please don't let me be sick."

She pulled herself into a sitting position and willed herself to get up. But as the day dragged on she felt worse and worse. At last she had to concede defeat and take to her bed.

Maybe if I rest today, I'll be fine by tomorrow, Emily hoped.

But she wasn't fine the next day. Her fever increased and her pulse raced. It was all she could do to make it from her bed to the kitchen.

I must drink fluids, she reminded herself, but it was difficult even to swallow.

She placed a pitcher of water and a glass beside her bed and again lay down.

"Please, God," she prayed feverishly, "make me well for Sunday." But when the first of the children arrived on Sunday morning, Emily was not there to open the door. They stood on the walk, wondering what to do.

Mrs. Reilly was the next to arrive. She greeted Sophie's four youngsters and chatted while they waited for Emily.

"It's strange," she murmured as the minutes ticked by. "I wouldn't expect her to be late."

"Maybe *her* cows got out," quipped young Nicky, and all the little cluster shared in the laughter.

Mrs. Travis arrived, her two children close behind her.

Mrs. Reilly greeted her warmly and then said, "It's strange, I wouldn't expect Emily to oversleep. It's past Sunday school hour." She fidgeted a few moments more and then moved resolutely toward Emily's gate.

"I'll just go see," she told the waiting group, and off she went to Emily's door.

There was no answer to her knock, and since there was no lock on the door Mrs. Reilly opened it and let herself in.

She found a very ill Emily. She could scarcely lift her head from her pillow, but she still fussed over the fact that she was not there to open the church building.

Mrs. Reilly sent Nicky for Dr. Andrew and tried to make Emily more comfortable in the meantime by putting a wet cloth on her forehead. There was nothing for Emily to do but to accept the ministrations. There would be no service that Sunday.

———

It took me nearly a week to get back on my feet, Emily wrote to Ruth. *I don't know what I would have done without Mrs. Reilly. She came every day to see how I was and to make sure I ate her nice, hot soup. Even Sophie from the cafe sent her Nicky over with a sandwich, and Mrs. Travis baked a loaf of bread for me.*

I don't dare write to my father about how sick I was, she continued, *or he would really be worried.* Emily finished her letter with words of enthusiasm for Ruth's fine progress and continued hope for her own situation.

Chapter Sixteen

Autumn

Other than the handful of women who had become her friends, Emily's adoption into the Wesson Creek community came slowly. She wished that Big John, as he was known in the area, didn't treat her quite so gruffly and that the young fellows did not loiter about the doors of the blacksmith shop staring at her as she walked to the post office or did her shopping. She wished the neighborhood women were more free to drop in for a cup of tea and that the young children didn't still dip their heads in shyness when she spoke to them.

"Be patient," she kept insisting to herself, but sometimes it was very hard to do so.

Gradually the attendance in the little church picked up. But just when Emily began to exult over the possibility of higher numbers, others would drop out.

"How do I keep them faithful? Consistent?" she lamented to the Lord. "I know I'm not a good preacher—but I try to make it interesting."

Letters from Ruth still included glowing reports of the growth in her church, though she too acknowledged a setback or two.

Things were even more difficult for Verna Woods, Emily concluded after reading her letter. The community where Verna served seemed to have less interest in church and spiritual matters than Wesson Creek. In fact, Verna was already admitting

125

that she often thought of giving up and going home. Emily sent her an encouraging note and prayed daily for Verna.

Emily knew several households quite well by now and that encouraged her.

Whenever she was passing, she dropped in on the lady who had no interest in "religious peddlers." She seemed so lonely that Emily ached for her. Emily didn't mention anything about church when she called there, though she longed to do so. She was sure she knew the cure for Clara's lonely heart. It was found in the pages of the Book Emily carried, tucked protectively in a corner of her buggy.

Soon the community was astir with harvesting activity. In the fields along the road, Emily observed teams of draft horses or chugging tractors from morn to dusk as she made her calls. Womenfolk took over the choring and cooked hardy meals, drawing on their abundant gardens. The children scurried to the fields with pails of fresh water or beef sandwiches and lemon tarts. Everyone was busy and Emily observed all the productive commotion as well as tension in the air as she visited the farm families. Every cloud was viewed with alarm. Would rain bring the harvesting to a standstill? Could there be a chance of snow?

Emily continued calling on folks, but she respected the harvesting situation. She certainly did not expect a farmwife to turn away from the pie crusts to prepare her visitor a cup of tea. She did not pause for polite conversation when a farmer was on his way to the granary with a wagonload of grain. Emily had grown up on a farm. She knew the pressure of the harvest.

Thus Emily decided to concentrate her efforts in town for the present. Sophie always seemed glad to see her, and cheerfully served her coffee and sat down to chat when she wasn't busy. Big John's sister at the mercantile, too, didn't seem to mind an occasional chat.

Also there was much to do around her own small place. While the harvesting was being completed, she busied herself cleaning up the weedy garden, patching her broken fences, repairing seams in aging dresses, and securing buttons on her winter coat.

She had more time for Bible study in preparation for future Sundays and caught up on her letter writing, baked cookies for an elderly lady down the street, and sewed a new, much-needed winter skirt.

She even took time for the luxury of a few walks in the woods. Beneath her feet the fallen leaves rustled with each footfall. Above, those that remained danced joyfully in the autumn breeze. Still higher in the sky, the Canada geese honked their goodbyes in V-formation as they flew their way to warmer climates. Other birds that would stay for the winter fluttered anxiously about to locate each berry tree, each rose bush, for future use. Squirrels scolded and bush rabbits ducked for cover when they saw her coming. Emily found great pleasure in the life of the woods.

Her feet always found their way back to the same spot—the cluster of trees along the creek where she had been resting the day she met Shad Austin. The creek had slowed further with the passing of summer. In some places it barely moved at all, but here, at the place Emily was sure was a favorite fishing hole, it still gurgled and played over stones as it left the small pond. Dragonflies zoomed in and out, and hornets settled on fallen leaves to ride a moment on the water.

Emily loved this restful little hideaway. Its peace refreshed her with each visit. On some days she brought her Bible and read as she basked in the serenity. Occasionally she wondered about the man whom she'd accidentally met in that place.

Mrs. Reilly had not mentioned the young man again. Emily did not wish to pry, but she often found herself trying to imagine what had brought about the change in his life. Why had he given up his calling and seemingly deserted his faith? What had happened to both of his parents that he was alone? *When* had it happened? Emily mulled over the questions as she watched the pond's activity.

Her thoughts always led her to prayer. Whatever the situation, she knew there was a need. She pictured the tears in Molly Reilly's eyes and heard again the words, "It would be an answer to his mother's prayers," and Emily added her voice to those prayers on Shad's behalf.

Emily met Mr. Travis for the first time when she went to get her team from the farm one day.

Claude was usually there to bring her horses. Though he was scarcely taller than Emily herself, he insisted on harnessing them. Emily allowed him to do so, assuming that he was likely being schooled by his mother to act the part of a gentleman. She had all she could do to keep from trying to help him as the lad struggled to lift the heavy harness over the backs of Star and Shadow.

On that particular day, instead of Claude, a man walked out to meet her.

"Mawnin'," he greeted, and touched his cap.

"Good morning," Emily responded, quickly making some deductions and extending her hand. "You're Mr. Travis?"

The man chuckled as he shook Emily's hand. "Been a long time since I been called mister."

Emily didn't quite understand his little joke, but she told him her name.

He nodded and said, "Ya wantin' yer team?" Emily assured him that she was.

"You go on in to see the missus an' I'll fetch 'em for ya," he said good-naturedly and Emily agreed.

He certainly was gaunt, she noted as she moved toward the house. His whiskered face seemed to sag in where his cheeks should be, and his clothing hung on his slight frame. He walked with a slow, lumbering step, and Emily wondered if he would have the strength to make it to the barn, let alone the pasture where the horses fed.

Oh, dear, she scolded herself, *should I be letting him exert himself this way?* Uncertain about what to do, she went on to the house.

Mrs. Travis welcomed her and put the teakettle on to boil.

"Hope you're not in too big a rush," she said slowly. "Claude is off to the neighbors and Wilbur might take a while getting your team."

"Should—should I have allowed him—?" began Emily and

then changed it to, "Is he well enough to deal with the horses?"

Mrs. Travis cast a glance at Emily. "He's fine," she said crisply. "Best he's been in some time."

Oh, my, thought Emily. *The poor man! If that is his best, he must have really been ill.*

The team eventually arrived at the door, and Emily bid Mrs. Travis goodbye and left. She felt even more concerned for the family. Over the months she had noted bruises on Mrs. Travis on more than one occasion and wondered if the woman needed to see Dr. Andrew about her continual falls.

"I do wish there were a way I could help. The poor man. Poor Mrs. Travis!" Emily said under her breath as she drove from the yard.

———

After that Emily often spotted Mr. Travis on the town streets. She realized she had seen him before without knowing who he was. On some days he could scarcely walk, and Emily wondered why he came into town when he was obviously so weak. Surely the man's precarious health should be guarded carefully. If his condition continued to deteriorate, the Travis family would soon be without a father.

Emily wondered if she should speak to anyone about the situation. Surely the townspeople were aware of what was going on. Didn't anyone care? Had anyone attempted to get help for the family? Had the man ever had medical attention?

Emily fretted but didn't know what she could do.

———

Carefully Emily counted her money. She was getting awfully low on funds. The Sunday offerings she had depended on amounted to only a few coins. *What can one expect when the congregation is mostly children?* she thought. She was very glad for the eggs and milk regularly supplied by Mrs. Reilly, but items such as salt, soap and flour had to be purchased at the mercantile. It was the lack of soap that had Emily concerned now.

Well, I must have it, she concluded. *I can't run around in dirty clothes.* Emily picked up her near-empty purse and headed for the store.

"Good morning," she greeted Big John cautiously. She had been hoping his sister would be minding the store. From the back rooms came the sound of activity, and Emily knew that Miss McMann was busy with housekeeping duties.

"Humph!" Big John snorted.

"I—I need some soap," stated Emily, giving up on conversation.

"What kind?" he snapped.

"For my laundry," responded Emily.

"Duz? Maple Leaf? Oxydol? Sunlight? Iv—?"

"What—which one is the cheapest?" Emily asked, embarrassed.

Big John swung around. "So ya bargain shop? Well, at least thet shows *some* sense." If he had not emphasized "some," Emily might have felt strangely complimented.

"How big a box?" he asked her as he reached for the soap. "Large or Family?"

"No—the—the small box—please," said Emily, her cheeks growing hotter.

"Thought ya was bargain smart," huffed Big John. "Now thet ain't wise buyin'."

"Mr.—Mr. John," Emily said, her voice more stern than she intended, "I would love to be a wise shopper. I know that one does save more by buying the larger box, but—I—I only buy what I can afford to pay for."

She dropped the money on his counter, spun on her heel and left the store with the soap, her head high.

How that man manages to rile me, she fumed and then felt guilty. She was there to show love—whether people were loving in return or not. She was the one who was to be gracious and forgiving. *I've failed again,* she mourned. She could never hope to win this neighbor if she responded that way. She turned around and went back into the store.

"Ferget somethin'?" Big John gruffly greeted her.

"Yes. Yes, I did," faltered Emily, her cheeks crimson, her

eyes bright with tears. "I—I forgot my manners. I forgot my Christian upbringing. My father would be embarrassed by my behavior, and I'm sure my—my heavenly Father is disappointed. I am sorry."

By the time Emily had finished her little speech, her voice was little more than a whisper. "Please—please forgive me," she asked, blinked back the tears, and left the man staring after her, his mouth open in astonishment.

Chapter Seventeen

Celebrations

I visited Bible school last week, Ruth wrote again, *and thought you would be interested in all the news. I hardly know where to start. Each time I heard another report about one of our classmates, I jotted it down so I wouldn't forget to tell you.*

Morris expects to leave for the mission field next May. He is so excited. He is going to Nigeria.

Word has it that the Russells are doing well in their pastorate at Conner. They are expecting their first child next April. Guess Agatha has not been at all well, so I do hope things soon improve for her. Poor Fred has had to be preacher and nurse and house-keeper all at the same time.

Olive broke off her engagement to Ross. I heard he was dev-astated. Seems that she and Robert Lee, her dear little Rob, are planning a December wedding. Hope they make it. Maybe they deserve each other.

Another engagement has also been announced. Lacey Beckett and Mary Frieson. I think they make a nice couple. Perhaps Mary will help to polish him up a bit.

But the biggest surprise for me was how much he has already changed—Lacey Beckett, our big, boyish Lacey. He seems so much more mature. And has such concern for others. I couldn't believe my eyes and ears. He is still planning on the ministry, and Pearl told me that Rev. Witt views him as the prize candidate for a new church work in the city. In the city, *mind you! Was a day when I thought the poor boy wouldn't even make it on the farm. God sure is full of surprises!*

Emily had to agree. "Isn't it amazing what God can do with a life given completely over to Him?" she murmured. Then she smiled, "Especially Lacey's—and mine!"

Ruth had other bits of information about faculty members and people they both had known. It was a long, newsy letter and it left Emily feeling very homesick for the school and those like Miss Herrington who had nurtured and loved her.

She wiped away unbidden tears as she folded up the letter and returned it to the envelope. Then she hastened to get out her pen and writing paper. She would write to Ruth while all the news was still fresh in her mind.

Mrs. Reilly was the first to mention the Harvest Picnic to Emily. "Of course you'll go," she declared. "Everyone does. It will be a wonderful opportunity for you to meet the neighborhood in a less formal way."

"I haven't even heard about it," said Emily. "Tell me more."

"We have it every year as soon as the harvesting is over. Everybody comes. It's at the fairgrounds. The meat is supplied by various farmers. We all take turns. Then everybody brings favorite dishes and potluck for the rest of the meal. It's great fun."

"It sounds fun," agreed Emily. She hadn't done anything just for fun in a long time.

"There are races and tugs-of-war and a ball game. Sometimes we even have booths for the kids. You know—balls to throw, a fish pond, apple dunking . . . things like that. They love it. It's the big event of the year."

"I'd love to go!" exclaimed Emily enthusiastically.

From then on the fall picnic came often to Emily's attention. Everywhere she went people were talking about it. Posters, made by the school children, began to turn up all over town. Word had it that Big John was going to provide some firecrackers for the event, and the farm kids were already coaxing their folks to stay late enough to be able to watch them.

Emily wondered what she should bring as her share of the meal. Her grocery supplies were depleting rapidly, and she still faced the long winter months.

Maybe I should take a trip home and get some more, she wondered, but it was such a long way to go and it was late enough in the fall that a winter storm could sweep in at any time. No, if she had been going to travel home for supplies, she should have done it weeks earlier.

She refused to write home to her father for money. She was sure he would send what he could if he knew of her plight, but she was on her own now—and serving the Lord. Didn't she believe that the Lord would provide? Where was her faith if she had to rush to her earthly father when the cupboard got a bit bare?

"Hold steady!" Emily often said to herself. "Be still, and know that He is God," she quoted from her beloved Bible.

But Emily had to admit that the coming event was a worry on her mind.

I have milk and eggs, she thought suddenly. "I'll make a custard," she announced, brightening.

That made Emily feel better, but she was sure she was expected to bring more than one dish. *I do have potatoes—and onions,* she mused. *I guess I'll just have to experiment.*

But Emily didn't feel too confident about experimentation when the community at large would be sampling her work.

———

On the day of the picnic Emily made her custard as planned and was pleased that it turned out just right. She sprinkled nutmeg over the top and turned to her experimental dish. She cooked a pot of potatoes and mashed them until they were light and fluffy, generously adding some of Mrs. Reilly's farm cream. Then she stirred in a few chopped onions. Last of all she whipped up some eggs, which she seasoned, then poured the mixture into the little pockets she had scooped in the potatoes in her pan.

"If I just had some cheese to sprinkle over the top," she murmured thoughtfully as she slid the pan into the oven.

A knock at her door turned out to be Mrs. Reilly.

"How are you coming?" she asked. "Ummm, that custard looks good."

"I've just popped my second dish into the oven," Emily responded cheerfully. Then she stopped short. "Oh no!" she wailed.

"What's wrong?" asked Mrs. Reilly anxiously.

"The supper—it won't be eaten till evening! Who will want to eat cold potatoes and eggs? I didn't think—"

Mrs. Reilly looked relieved. "Is that all," she said, waving aside Emily's consternation. "Don't worry about it. Keep it for your Sunday dinner. You can rewarm it later. Anyway, the custard is more than your fair share. There's always much more food than can ever be eaten. I've got to run. I'm helping with the ice cream. Here's your milk and eggs. And there's a bit of cheese there, too. George's sister brought me a great wedge of it. We'll never manage to eat it all on our own."

Cheese! Emily's eyes opened wide.

"Now don't be late," the older woman admonished as she hurried off.

———

Emily prepared herself carefully for the outing. She chose her prettiest housedress, pinned up her hair extra carefully, and for a long moment debated about her deaconess bonnet. Should or shouldn't she wear it? Would the parishioners expect to see her appear properly attired as the town mission worker, or would she look foolish attending a picnic in her ministry garb?"

At last Emily laid her bonnet back on the shelf. She would go without the hat.

———

She could smell her cookery as she entered her kitchen to lift the hot pan from the oven. Emily was tempted to try a small forkful of the food.

It *was* tasty. She scraped a few shreds of cheese onto another mouthful and took another bite. That made it even better. *Just one more bite,* she decided. It was good. Really good.

"Oh, dear," she giggled. "I won't be able to enjoy any of that beef if I don't quit!" Emily paused long enough to pick up her custard and grab her coat in case the evening was chilly, then left excitedly for the town fairgrounds.

Emily couldn't remember when she had last had so much fun. She shared in the laughter as the sack racers toppled and scrambled for the finish line. She licked ice cream that ran down her cone before it could spill on her hands, she shouted encouragement to her Sunday school students as they took part in the wheelbarrow race, and cheered on the softball players. She even tried her hand at dunking for apples, soaking her face and the curls that framed it. The children laughed and squealed their delight when she tossed the ball that sent the mayor of the town into the dunk tank and urged her to try her hand at it again with the schoolteacher.

Before she knew it, it was time for the picnic supper.

Emily stood in line with Sophie's Olivia on one side and little Rena Travis on the other. The food smelled delicious in spite of her sampling from the potato dish.

The line was long, and the two children got fidgety.

"Go ahead," urged Emily when they saw an opportunity to dart ahead and join their own family members. "Your mothers are waiting for you."

Emily stood near the end of the line, humming softly to herself. This was the first time she had really felt a part of the small community.

"How's the preacher?" a voice asked at her elbow.

Which one of those young fellows is teasing me now? Emily's thought as her head came around. *They still laugh and jostle and throw out silly dares to one another whenever I come in sight.*

But it was Shad Austin who stood next to her, a teasing smile on his lips.

"If you are referring to me—I'm just fine," she answered evenly.

His eyes conveyed an apology, though he did not express it aloud. "Actually, Aunt Moll sent me to get you. There's an extra spot at the table over there. She said to tell you to join us."

"Thank you," Emily replied and moved up a step in the line.

He followed her. Emily noticed that he carried an empty plate.

"I didn't realize you were here," Emily commented for something to say.

"I never miss the Harvest Picnic," he said. "I've been here most of the afternoon."

Emily wondered fleetingly where he had been and why she hadn't seen him.

"I was manning the dunk tank," he continued, laughing. "I helped you dunk the mayor," he remarked.

"But I—I thought the ball did that when—" began Emily.

"It should—if it's working. Ours doesn't work quite right. So someone has to be underneath to pull the rope and tip the seat."

"Oh-h," laughed Emily. "I didn't think I was that good a shot. Well, thanks for the help."

He smiled. "I just hope the mayor doesn't find out who was responsible," he quipped.

The line moved by tables weighted with the community's bounty. Emily was faced with some difficult choices.

"That's Mrs. Long's potato salad," Shad offered. "She makes the best salad I've ever tasted." Or, "Mrs. Tennet's pumpkin pie. I'm surprised there's any left," and again, "I knew it. Not a scrap of Mr. Willmore's fudge cookies."

"Mr. Willmore's?"

"He brings them every year."

Emily chuckled. She couldn't imagine the no-nonsense schoolteacher standing over a hot oven baking fudge cookies.

"Which dish did you bring?" Shad wanted to know. Emily pointed out the custard, and he helped himself to the last serving.

When they had their plates filled to capacity, Shad directed her to the table where George and Molly Reilly ate with several neighbors.

Emily was content to sit and listen to the chatter and laughter. Occasionally a question was directed her way and she answered pleasantly.

"So what do you think of our Harvest Picnic?" a big farmer in bib overalls and a white shirt asked her.

"I love it," she answered honestly. "I haven't had so much fun since I was a school kid."

"I agree," enthused Molly Reilly. "I think we should have community picnics more often."

"Guess the next big social event is the school Christmas program," said a woman at the end of the table.

And so the talk and laughter continued. Emily snuggled into the warmth of belonging and wished that the evening could go on and on.

But eventually the women began to gather pots and dishes and the menfolk moved to take down the tables and load them on Eric Thorn's farm truck. One by one families with young children began to leave, the little ones whining at missing the fireworks.

Emily gathered her own things under a nearby poplar. A soft darkness was beginning to steal across the open fairgrounds. With the night came a coolness and Emily buttoned her coat.

"Did you bring a blanket?" Mrs. Reilly called as she walked by, looking for a suitable place on the ground.

"I thought you'd gone," answered Emily. "No. I didn't even think of a blanket."

"Well, come share mine," the woman offered, "and no, I didn't go. Shad drove George home to do the chores."

So Shad is gone. For a brief moment Emily felt a twinge of disappointment. Then she quickly put the thought out of her mind and went to catch up to Molly.

As soon as Big John was satisfied that it was dark enough to properly show off his fireworks, he sent the first one whistling into the sky. Emily had never watched such a display before, and she thrilled at the burst of sparkling color.

She was clapping enthusiastically with the crowd when she heard, "Are you warm enough?"

Emily looked up to discover that Shad had returned. He sat down beside her, situating himself to shield her from the cool night wind.

"I'm fine," whispered Emily, not sure why she whispered. Others were shouting or cheering with every new explosion of color and light.

All too soon the display ended and Emily found herself shivering. She wasn't sure if it was from excitement or cold. She stood to her feet and pulled her coat more tightly about her small frame.

You'll be sick, her father's voice played in her memory, and Emily prayed fervently that it might not be so.

"Can you come for dinner tomorrow?" Mrs. Reilly was asking as she folded up her blanket.

"I'd like that," Emily admitted. She had eaten with the Reilly's a number of times and always enjoyed it.

"Good. We'll see you after church."

And then Mrs. Reilly was gone, leaving Emily standing with Shad.

"Come on," he said, taking her arm. "I'll drive you home."

Emily eased her elbow from his hand. *Aren't you being a bit presumptuous?* she could have asked. *Not "may I," or "do you mind?" but "I'll drive you home."*

But Emily walked with Shad to his car and accepted the lift. The night was cool, her coat inadequate—and his company pleasing.

Chapter Eighteen

Troubles and Woes

The attendance at the worship service the next morning was down. Emily was sure that many of the children, and perhaps some of the adults, had found it a little more difficult to get up after yesterday's celebrations.

But George and Molly Reilly were there for Sunday school. Emily had let herself wonder if Shad would accompany them and worried about how it might affect her presentation of the lesson if he did.

"Shad volunteered to do the chores to give George the morning off," Molly volunteered, and Emily felt both disappointed and relieved.

After the service Molly approached Emily as she re-stacked hymnbooks. "I'm going to scoot on home and see to dinner," she said. "I'll send Shad in for you in half an hour or so."

Emily could only nod in agreement.

She finished tidying the small church and dumped the coins from the offering plate into the palm of her hand. She had been hoping for a bill or two—she was low on so many things she needed. And then she chided herself. She was not serving for the money. Times had been tough for everyone. The whole community was still feeling the effects of the recent drought. This was the first decent crop year for many of the area farmers, and Emily could well imagine that they had a lot of debts of their

141

own. *I can't look to them for what I need any more than I can to my father,* she decided firmly.

"My God shall supply all your needs," she quoted aloud as she returned to her quarters to freshen up before her dinner engagement.

Shad arrived in the half hour stated and Emily was ready and waiting.

"How about bringing along walking shoes?" he suggested. "We might feel like a visit to the creek this afternoon."

Emily tried to keep the flush from her cheeks and went to get her other shoes.

"It's a beautiful fall day," Shad remarked as he reached for the shoes Emily carried. "It might be the last opportunity to take a walk before the winter snows come."

Emily agreed with a nod, waiting while Shad held the door of his car for her.

Shad broke the silence.

"Have you been out to Wesson Creek lately?"

Emily was puzzled. "I *live* in Wesson Creek," she reminded him, feeling a little silly but not knowing what else to say.

Shad smiled. "I mean the real Wesson Creek," he responded, and Emily suddenly knew what he meant.

"Oh-h—the creek. Is that what it's called?"

Shad nodded and Emily chuckled. "It makes perfect sense, doesn't it? I just hadn't heard it called by name before."

"So?" he asked. "Have you been back?"

"Many times," Emily admitted. "I go there as often as I can."

She blushed, hoping Shad didn't think her trips to the creek had anything to do with him.

"So do I," Shad stated simply. "Ever since I was a kid."

"It's so—so peaceful there. Sort of—sort of like being in church," Emily dared to say.

She saw a slight shadow pass over Shad's face, but all he said was, "The most peaceful spot I know."

Dinner with the Reillys was enjoyable for Emily, who often ate alone. Shad seemed to fit well in the family of George and Molly. Emily thought it was a shame Molly had not had children herself, but certainly Shad acted as if he belonged.

After Emily had helped Molly with the dishes, Shad suggested they take their walk and Emily nodded in agreement and changed her shoes.

From the Reilly farm it was not as far to the creek as it was from where Emily lived in town, and soon the two were approaching the special pond.

Shad tossed his jacket over a fallen log and motioned for Emily to sit there. He flopped down on the grass beside the small stream.

"It's almost dry in some spots," he said as if to himself. "When I was a boy, it often overflowed its banks. The drought has changed that, but it's coming back now," he added on a more hopeful note.

"Those years were hard on everyone—everything," murmured Emily, watching the leaves floating on the surface. "I'm glad they're over."

"I'm not really sure they are," Shad surprised her by saying.

But he quickly changed the subject. "So where did you grow up?" he questioned, and the rest of the afternoon was spent exchanging bits of information. Emily found herself telling him about her father, Ina and Annabelle. She talked of her school years and her home church and even shared some about her two years at the Bible school.

They walked slowly back to the Reilly farm, feet shuffling through the autumn leaves, laughter coming easily as they shared a joke. Emily had never experienced an afternoon quite like it before.

As they came to the rails that divided the farmyard from the pasture land, Shad spoke softly to Emily. "I owe you an apology for the smart-alecky way I acted on the day we met by the creek."

Emily turned to look at him. "Oh, but—" she began, but he lifted a hand.

"But I do," he continued. "I had no reason to tease you as I did. I've felt sorry about it ever since."

"Really, I—I've thought nothing more of it," Emily fumbled.

"Well, I have—with embarrassment. Do you suppose we could sort of—start over?"

Emily laughed then, a merry, good-humored sound. "Well, I guess we have," she stated.

Shad smiled. "You'll forgive me?"

Emily's eyes sparkled as she turned to the young man and reached out a small hand to his. "Forgiven," she said simply, and Shad accepted the proffered hand and held it after the shake until he had helped her through the rail fence.

Back at the farmhouse, Molly had coffee ready. Emily didn't think she was hungry, but when she tasted the sandwiches, they were so good that she ate two of them.

The talk around the table was cheerful and lively and Emily wished it could go on forever.

"As much as I hate to," Shad finally said, "I've got to head back to Calgary. It'll be late by the time I get there."

Emily had not thought of him driving back that night.

George nodded his agreement. "Don't want you fallin' asleep on the way," he said, and Molly looked toward him with concern.

"I won't," Shad quickly assured her. "But I do need to get going." Then he turned to Emily. "If you're ready," he offered, "I'll drive you home."

Emily hurried to get her purse and her extra pair of shoes.

"I could walk," she told him as they started for his car. "It's not far and it would do me good."

"And deny me the privilege?" he teased.

"Well, it would save you some time," she continued.

"I'm not *that* pressed for time. It'll only take a few minutes to drive into town," he said as he helped her into the car.

After a moment or two of peaceful quiet, Shad said, "I'm not sure when I will get out again. Maybe not until Christmas."

"I'm hoping to go home at Christmastime," Emily said, thinking wistfully of her family.

Shad was silent, and Emily could sense that something was wrong.

"Yes!" Shad finally said softly. "I hope you can. Your family must really miss you."

Emily realized then that he had been wondering about seeing her again, and she had unthinkingly slammed the door on the possibility. She did not know what to say next.

"Of course, I will need to be here for Christmas Sunday," she said slowly.

He was quick to pick up the slightest invitation. "Maybe I could drive you home," he suggested almost shyly.

Emily felt her pulse quicken. It sounded almost like a date. What would her father think about her bringing a man home who did not share their faith? No, she could not do that. To take Shad home with her would be like acknowledging that he was her beau. And even beyond her father's concerns were her own. *I cannot think of him in that way—ever,* she told herself. There was no way she could accept the company of a non-Christian man except as a friend.

"I—I will need to do a great deal of praying about that," responded Emily.

Silence hung heavy about them.

"I take that as a no," Shad said softly.

"I guess it is," spoke Emily, nervously clasping her hands on her lap. "It isn't that I wouldn't like to say yes."

"I understand."

Emily wondered if he really did. She was near to tears and hoped fervently that he wouldn't notice.

When they arrived at the little church, Shad held Emily's car door for her. She gathered her purse and her shoes and climbed out slowly. She hated for things to end this way, but there seemed nothing else she could do.

"I enjoyed the day," Shad was saying close to her ear.

"I did, too," Emily echoed. She felt near to tears again.

"Goodbye, Emily."

But Emily choked on her answer. She hated to say goodbye, for she knew how final this goodbye would be. She didn't say, "Can't we just be friends?" for she knew instinctively that they both wished for more than friendship.

She blinked back the tears that threatened to fall, managed a wobbly smile and said a soft "Thank you" before leaving.

———

Emily was nearly blinded by tears as she stumbled down

the walk leading to her door. She had heard the car reverse and then leave the front of the church. Shad was on his way back to the city. That was as it should be. That was as it *had* to be, but Emily couldn't deny the ache in her heart. She had never felt this way about a man before.

She was about to reach for her doorknob when she stumbled over something. Her eyes looked through the darkness for the cause and a gasp escaped her lips. It was Mr. Travis, collapsed on her doorstep! *Maybe he had been coming to me for help while I was out spending a frivolous day mooning over a man I can not have.* Frantic thoughts raced through her mind.

Emily dropped her shoes and purse and leaned over the man. He smelled of vomit. Emily felt both revolted and frightened. *He must be very ill. I have to get help right away.*

It was too far to Dr. Andrew's. She ran to the closest person.

"Mr. John! Mr. John!" she cried, beating loudly with her fist on the mercantile door. "Please. Please! Let me in."

When the door opened, Big John stood there, a slice of unfinished bread and butter in his hand, his jaws still working on the last bite he had taken.

"What is it?" he asked, concern in his voice. But Emily was shaking so hard she could not speak.

He tossed the unfinished bread onto a nearby counter and grasped Emily by the shoulders.

"What is it?" he asked again.

Emily found her voice then. "It's—it's Mr. Travis."

Big John's eyes flew wide. He steadied Emily with one huge hand and studied her trembling lips. "What did he do to ya?" he asked sternly.

"No—no, not to me. He—he's sick. He collapsed—on my doorstep. Quickly—he needs help."

Big John strode toward the door. He still had not released Emily's arm, and she scrambled to keep up.

Mr. Travis was lying right where she had left him.

Emily pointed one shaky finger. "He's—he's fainted or collapsed or something."

Big John pushed her back and stepped deliberately in front of her as he moved forward, stopping by the fallen man.

"He's stinkin' drunk," he hissed as he bent over him. "He's stinkin' drunk like he always is."

Emily gasped. She had never encountered a man in Mr. Travis's condition.

"The scum," hissed Big John again, raising to his feet and pushing the inert man's arm to his side with a booted foot. "If he weren't on yer doorstep, I'd leave him right where he is." And Big John spat in the grass.

"Is—is he often like—like this?" faltered Emily.

"Only on the weekdays an' every weekend," responded the big man with a sarcastic growl.

"What about—what about Mrs. Travis? Does she know?" whispered Emily as though she were afraid her remark might betray the secret.

Big John looked at her steadily. "I guess she knows," he said deliberately; "seein' how he knocks her around whenever he can stand up straight."

Emily's breath caught in her throat.

"Where ya been all yer life, kid?" John asked gruffly. "Where'd ya think she got all those bruises? Runnin' into doors?"

Emily just shook her head. *So—so the whole town knows the truth, and I never guessed. Poor, poor Mrs. Travis,* she thought to herself.

Big John hoisted the fallen man to his back and carried him off down the walk.

Emily picked up her purse and shoes, stepped across the vomit on her walk and let herself in her door. She felt sick herself as she carried a pail of water out to slosh her step clean once again.

Later, Big John was back. Without a word he went to work, placing a sturdy lock on Emily's door. Emily watched in silence.

When he finished, he lifted his eyes to hers. "An' see thet ya use it," he said, and then was gone.

Chapter Nineteen

Winter

Emily felt awkward and ill-at-ease the next time she had to go to the Travis farm to pick up her team. Mrs. Travis waved her usual greeting and called to see if Emily had time to stop for tea. She wished she could decline but really had no excuse. She found it difficult to converse naturally with the older woman now that she knew the dreadful secret.

Emily even found herself inspecting the woman's face to determine if she had any new bruises. She caught herself, lowered her eyes in shame and prayed silently that God would help her to show the same love and concern for Mrs. Travis and her children as she had previously done. Yes, and for Mr. Travis, too.

The children greeted Emily just as warmly as ever, and that helped her to feel a bit more relaxed.

Rena crowded up against Emily's skirts and showed her the new kitten she had discovered in the barn.

"Would you like a kitten?" Rena asked generously as Emily's hand stroked the soft fur.

"I love kittens," Emily confided, "but I'm not sure it would be a good idea for me to have one at the parsonage."

"Why? She could eat your mice."

Emily cringed. She did hate the mice that plagued her small home. "Does she already hunt mice?"

"Well—no, not yet. But she will when she gets bigger. Her

149

mommy catches lots of mice. I always see her taking one to her babies," Rena went on, her pale blue eyes full of the immensity of her knowledge.

Emily's hand moved from the kitten to the head of the child. *What a beautiful little thing she would be if she had dainty hair ribbons and prettier clothes,* thought Emily, and immediately checked herself. Mrs. Travis was doing all she could for her little family. It was impossible for her to do more under her trying circumstances.

Timmie came over and lifted the kitten from Rena's arms. "I should take her back," he explained softly to his sister. "She might be hungry again." Then he turned to Emily. "There are three others at the barn if you'd like to choose one." Then he added hurriedly, "They have to grow for a couple more weeks, and then they'll be ready to eat from a dish."

"I'll think about it," Emily promised with a warm smile. She did have plenty of milk from Mrs. Reilly—and if the kitten would be a good mouser, she might be worth her keep at the parsonage. Emily would enjoy the company, without doubt.

Winter came softly to the land. Emily had retired one night with feathery flakes drifting slowly down from the heavens and awoke the next morning to a world of white. It was a beautiful sight, the morning sun making the whole drab world outside Emily's kitchen window one glorious wonderland.

Midafternoon it began to snow again and continued on throughout the evening and into the night. By the next morning Emily had eight inches of fluffy snow on her walks. It was Sunday, and Emily did not want her little congregation struggling through the new snowfall to reach her church door.

As she swept vigorously with her kitchen broom, a voice from behind her said, "Hi! Need some help?" It was Nicky, Sophie's oldest.

"Mom spotted ya," he said with a grin. "She said ya won't get nowhere with that." He pointed at the broom in her hands.

Emily smiled. "It's all I have. Hadn't even thought to prepare myself with a shovel."

"I've got one," said Nicky, holding a battered but serviceable shovel out for Emily to see. "I'll shovel and you sweep behind me."

Emily thought it was a good plan. They worked as a team, their breath puffing out before them in little silvery clouds.

"Look," called Nicky, "I'm a dragon."

Emily shared in his laughter.

In the weeks ahead, winter was no longer kind to the folks of the town and community of Wesson Creek. Emily watched the snow become deeper and deeper in the piles beside her walk. Each time she shovelled more onto the pile, she thanked the Lord for His answer to her prayer for a shovel of her own. One day, quite unexpectedly, she had spotted a handle protruding from the snow by the backyard fence. Emily tugged and pulled until a shovel made an appearance. She hadn't noticed it earlier in the year because she didn't need it. She couldn't help but say "Thank you, Lord!" right then and there. But then she took a closer look. The handle was broken. It had been put back together, but the patching too had cracked.

At first Emily had felt keen disappointment, but then she brightened at a sudden idea. Maybe for a few of her precious coins, she could buy a new handle. She would pay a visit to the store next door.

Big John McMann stood behind the counter. Emily didn't dread seeing him as much as she had in the past. He was still gruff and curt and still plagued her with jests and testing each time that they did business, but Emily sensed a softening in his demeanor.

"Good morning," she said brightly as she approached his counter.

"Whatcha got?" he growled in return.

"I've been in need of a shovel," said Emily, her eyes reflecting her excitement. "I found this one by the back fence. Can the handle be fixed—or replaced?"

"Fixed, no. But replaced, no problem."

"How much would a handle be?" asked Emily timidly.

"Let's see it," said Big John, and Emily struggled to lift the shovel across the counter.

"Reckon I could put on a new one fer fifty cents," he growled.

"*You* will fix it?" Emily could scarcely believe her ears. She'd been sure she would need to do the replacing herself, though she had no idea how to go about it, and certainly had no tools if it required that.

"Comes with the price of the handle," said Big John, not even lifting his eyes.

"I'll—I'll take it," responded Emily and opened her purse to carefully count out the coins.

But Big John did not hold out his hand for the change.

"Why don't ya jest throw those coins in the offerin' on Sunday?"

Emily could not believe her ears. She looked at the big man uncertainly. He stared back at her.

"Don't believe none in this here gospel-stuff," he hastened to inform Emily, "but always did like to carry a bit of insurance."

Emily's mouth dropped open, her eyes grew big, and then she slowly laid the change on the counter.

"I'm afraid this Policy is all or nothing, Mr. John. It's not insurance—it's assurance." She held his eyes steadily.

Big John reached down, picked up the coins and tossed them into his till. He still said nothing, nor did Emily.

"I'll have it ready fer ya to pick up in the mornin'," he finally said with a nod toward the shovel in his hands.

"Thank you," replied Emily softly. "I appreciate that," and she quietly left the store.

———

The winter temperatures dropped until Emily spent most of some days hauling in wood so she could keep her little house warm and have the small church somewhat comfortable for Sundays. She was alarmed that the woodpile she had considered so huge was rapidly decreasing in size. But Mr. Reilly noticed too and told her not to be concerned. He was arranging with neighborhood men to add to the pile in plenty of time to meet Emily's need.

What did worry Emily was the depletion of her food supplies. Her vegetables, carefully stored in the cellar beneath her kitchen, were nearly gone. But it was her nearly empty cupboard that gave her the most concern. By now it was not at all uncommon for women of the community to drop in for a warming cup of tea or coffee after a cold drive to town. Emily welcomed the opportunity to show hospitality. Some of the women who came did not attend church, and Emily felt the visits were a wonderful time for them to get to know one another better and perhaps give her occasion to share her faith in a nonthreatening setting.

But these visits were hard on her resources. Still she was determined that the women would always be welcome, that she would always try to supply them with tea—or coffee—to warm them and, as long as possible, a cookie or piece of cake to enjoy with the hot drink.

The flour was the first to give out. Then the sugar crock emptied—except for one cupful that Emily set aside for her visitors who took sugar with their cup of tea. Emily was glad she always had cream. Mrs. Reilly kept her in constant supply of milk and eggs.

Emily was also thankful for the eggs. She never needed to go hungry as long as she had eggs in the house—she cooked eggs as many ways as she knew how.

"If I can just manage at least tea and coffee until I go home for Christmas," Emily said to herself over and over. "Then Father will see to it that I get some supplies again."

Emily was looking forward to Christmas and seeing her family again. It would be wonderful to just relax away from all her responsibilities. She loved the work, but it was a constant drain on all her reserves.

She had planned a children's Christmas program. All her Sunday school children were involved and met at the church for practice after school on Tuesdays and again on Saturdays. Along with all the rest of Emily's duties, rehearsals certainly made her days busy. She prayed for continued health so she could keep up to the strenuous schedule. Just carrying in the wood to heat the church on so many occasions was a constant chore.

Emily felt a cold coming on, but she fought against it with all her strength and managed to keep going.

The night of the program arrived, and Emily was very pleased to see her small congregation of between ten and fifteen grow to thirty-nine.

Oh, if only we could have the church this full all the time! she enthused, carefully studying the audience to see where she needed to concentrate her calling on people after the Christmas season.

As Emily swept and tidied the little church the next day, she felt happier than she had for weeks. The program had been a great success. The children who took part had been so happy with the enthusiasm of the crowd. Those who had attended the little church for the first time seemed quite delighted with the evening. Emily could see great possibilities for growth now that more of the community had been introduced to the small congregation. Perhaps after Christmas there would be a real upswing in progress.

Christmas! Such a beautiful, powerful word to Emily. She stopped her sweeping, thrilled at the thought that God had actually given His Son. What a wonderful love gift to the world—to her.

Christmas! A time to see family again. Emily suddenly realized just how homesick she was. She had not really allowed herself to think of it before, but she missed her father. She missed Ina and Annabelle. She missed her familiar room, the warm coziness of the farmhouse kitchen, the security of warm fires and full cupboards and no responsibilities to make the provision. Emily could scarcely wait to reach home again. Her family was coming for her by car on the morrow, and she would have a full week at home before returning to the duties of the Wesson Creek parish.

After finishing her work in the little church, Emily returned to her rooms in a dreamy mood. With a thoughtful smile she took up her purse with its few cents and slipped into her coat and boots.

Miss McMann was busy adding stock to the shelves. Emily called a greeting, and the woman turned. "Feelin' cheery, ain't ya," she commented, but she didn't appear to share Emily's holiday spirit.

"I get to go home for Christmas tomorrow," Emily offered in explanation, and the woman nodded. But no smile filled her eyes.

Emily presented a short list of items and held her breath while the woman totalled the amount. Emily sighed with relief when she found she would be able to cover the cost of the purchases. She counted out the coins. She had two thin dimes left—but it was enough. Emily picked up her small bag of items and left happily for the parsonage.

In her warm little kitchen, Emily set to work at once, snatches of "O Little Town of Bethlehem" coming from her lips as she worked. Sophie and Mrs. Travis had always been so kind to her. She would say her thank you at this Christmas season by doing some baking for their children.

When the cookies had cooled, Emily decorated them with the resourcefulness of the creative in strained circumstances. When she was done she smiled at the snowmen, angels and holly wreaths. They looked rather cute in spite of the little with which she had to work. She hoped the children would enjoy them, and Emily carefully bundled up her little offerings of love and set out.

At Sophie's cafe she found the place bristling with activity. Sophie was so busy serving coffee and pie that Emily herself picked up the pot and for a half hour scrambled back and forth to keep up with the customers.

When at last the Christmas shoppers had drifted back out to the street, Sophie brushed back her hair with a weary hand and invited Emily to share a cup of coffee.

"I'd love to," said Emily, "but I need to get out to the Travises. I have some cookies for the children, and if I don't make it there soon, I'll be walking in the dark."

"Would ya like Nicky to go with ya?" offered Sophie.

"Oh no. No, I'll be just fine. I've walked that road so often I'm sure I could walk it in the dark if I had to," Emily assured her and shrugged into her coat.

Sophie surprised her by giving her a quick hug. "Thanks for the cookies," she whispered. "The kids'll love 'em. I never seem to get time to do anything special for 'em."

Emily smiled and returned the hug warmly.

Walking briskly to the Travis farm, Emily noticed the air was colder and a wind was stirring the bare branches of the trees along the road. The sun had disappeared behind a heavy cloud cover. Emily increased her speed.

But as Emily hastened up the drive toward the Travis home, she heard a commotion coming from the farmhouse. Angry shouts were followed by shrieks of an even more intense nature. Emily stopped mid-stride, not knowing what she should do.

"Don't go in there," a muffled voice warned from the shadows, and Emily turned to see Rena cowering in a corner of the shrubbery, a skimpy blanket pressed tightly around her slight body.

Emily hurried to the child and drew the little body close to her. Rena shivered as Emily held her, and Emily wasn't sure if it was from fright or the cold.

"You can't stay out here," Emily whispered. "You'll freeze."

"I—I can't go in," chattered the child.

"But—" began Emily and then asked instead. "Where are Claude and Timmie?"

"Claude ran away from home—last week," said the child simply. "I—I think Timmie might be in the barn—or the chicken coop."

Emily pulled her closer. The noise from the house intensified.

Something must be done. But what? Emily prayed as she stood helplessly, sheltering the child.

Sudden silence. Then the door opened and a tight, sobbing voice called out into the gathering darkness, "Rena. Timmie. You can come in. Rena."

"Guess Pa's sleepin' now," shivered Rena through tightly

clenched teeth, and she stirred in Emily's arms.

Emily felt tears streaming down her own cheeks. She brushed at them with the back of her mittened hand. *How can they live like this?* she wondered and let the little girl go.

"Timmie," came the call again.

Emily could see Mrs. Travis standing in the open doorway. Her dress was torn at the waistline and the skirt sagged sloppily into the snow on the doorstep. Her hair was dishevelled and, even from where Emily stood, she could see a small stream of blood as it coursed its way down and over the cheekbone. Mrs. Travis raised a shaky hand to wipe at it with the kitchen towel she held.

"Mrs. Travis," Emily called in a whispery voice as she led small Rena toward the woman. "May I help you? You could spend the night—" But the woman silenced her with a quick wave of her hand.

"We'll be all right now. He's sleepin'. He'll be okay in the mornin'," and she reached out to pull her shaking daughter into her own arms.

Emily hesitated, then knew that the woman needed to get back to her kitchen to tend to her own wounds. And Rena needed to be tucked close to the fire to chase the chill from her little bones.

Emily stepped back and turned to go. "I'll—I'll be praying for you," she whispered, but it seemed such a weak, empty promise to make under such circumstances. Emily drew a deep, shaky breath and turned away.

Timmie was coming toward her from the barn. He too was not dressed to be outdoors on a wintry night. Hay clung to his clothing and hair, and Emily guessed that he had burrowed his way into the hay in an effort to keep warm—or hidden.

Emily suddenly remembered her errand. She still had the package of cookies in her hand.

"I forgot," she said to the small boy. "I came to give you these—to wish you a—a Merry Christmas." Emily could scarcely choke the last words from her throat. A Merry Christmas? Hardly. Not with what Emily had just witnessed.

Timmie took the offered gift and in spite of his circumstance, he smiled and thanked her politely.

Emily turned from the small boy and directed her steps toward the road and home. The tears running freely down her face were soon frozen upon her cheeks.

How frightful! Emily mourned to herself. *What fear and pain they live with! Oh, God, there must be some way to help them. There must. Show us. Show me what we can do.*

Christmas! The most beautiful, special time of year—and they lived with abuse and suffering. Sobs choked Emily's throat.

It seemed that Mr. Travis had his own unique way of celebrating.

Chapter Twenty

Mixed Blessings

The next day a message came to Emily by way of Miss McMann. Emily was at her kitchen table, her small valise packed, her coat and hat nearby. She was dressed and ready to leave for home when the car arrived to pick her up.

At the sound of the knock on her door she rose to her feet, smiling softly to herself, and grabbed her coat as she went to bid a welcome to whichever member of her family had come to fetch her.

She was startled to see Miss McMann, but she quickly regained her composure and smiled.

"Come in," she offered. "Please come in. I'm expecting my ride anytime. They are sending over a car to take me home for Christmas. I thought that—"

But Miss McMann interrupted. "Thet's why I came. A call jest came. Yer father telephoned and asked if we'd tell ya thet they're delayed. Something's the matter with the car. They have to fix it before they can come. It won't be till tomorrow."

Emily was deeply disappointed. She had so counted on today. She had everything ready. She had nothing more that needed to be done. She—why, whatever would she do with another day on her hands? Besides, tomorrow was the twenty-fourth. Christmas Eve. She had wanted to be there to help Ina and Annabelle with the last-minute preparations for Christmas.

Emily turned back to Miss McMann, her shawl wrapped carelessly about her shoulders, her hair still sprinkled with quickly disappearing snowflakes.

"Thank you. Thank you for trudging through the snow to bring me word," she said and even managed a smile. "Would you have a cup of tea?" she offered rather awkwardly. Emily immediately remembered that she had just disposed of the last few drops of cream.

"I have to get back to the store," Miss McMann answered. "John is away."

Emily thanked her again and the woman left, promising Emily that she would one day come again. The promise brought a stir of excitement to Emily's disappointed heart. Miss McMann had not as yet been to Emily's house for tea.

But after the woman left, Emily felt the tears fill her eyes. She brushed impatiently at them with the back of her hand.

Don't be a child, she scolded herself. *You can wait until tomorrow. Get busy and find something to do.*

Emily looked around her small home. Everything was in place. Her simple furnishings were easy to keep in order. A good supply of wood lined the wall of her small entry. She had also carried an ample supply for the little church. There was no need to carry more.

She could not bake. Her cupboard was once again empty of flour, and only the one little bit of tea-sugar remained. The two dimes in her purse were not sufficient to buy more.

I'll go over to Sophie's and see what I can do, she determined. She pulled her coat over her traveling dress and left a note on her door concerning her whereabouts if her ride should come early.

She was about to leave when she thought, *What if I get to cleaning or baking at Sophie's?* She decided she'd better change into something more practical.

She was glad she had, for after explaining her predicament to Sophie and sharing a quick cup of hot apple cider, Emily entered the upstairs living quarters and set to work with the children, cleaning house and making simple decorations for the Christmas tree. Then they worked together to bake sugar cookies. By then the cafe had closed and Sophie joined them. They shared a supper of pancakes, shaped like little animals and snowmen, and by the time Emily had helped Sophie with the dishes and read a story to the children, it was late.

The day turned out well, after all, she smiled to herself as she let herself in the door. *And tomorrow I get to go home.*

The wind, which had blown all day, rattled the loose pipe that fed Emily's rain barrel, and made the gate creak on its hinges. She snuggled more closely under her blankets and prayed that the Travis children might be safely tucked into their beds, not cowering in some corner where the wind tore at their clothing . . . and then she fell asleep.

The wind was still blowing the next morning. Emily hastily prepared and ate a simple breakfast. She had no milk or cream, having disposed of her supply in preparation for being gone, so she again ate eggs—and eggs without anything else. *Oh, well,* she thought, *I'll soon be home for a turkey dinner.*

But as Emily washed her few dishes and tidied her small kitchen, Miss McMann knocked at her door. Another message had come. The roads had drifted closed. The car was unable to make it through. They felt so bad. They would miss her.

She would not make it home for Christmas.

For one moment Emily thought of her strong team of horses. They could drag her buggy through the drifts. If she left immediately she could make it home Christmas night. She might even make it for—but Emily checked herself. It was a foolish idea. She could well freeze in the process or lose her way in the storm.

She nodded her head and mumbled her thanks to Miss McMann. She did not even extend an invitation to tea as she knew she should. The woman seemed to understand and hurried from her door.

Emily did not fight the tears this time. She sank into the chair by the table, laid her head on her folded arms and cried until her whole body shook.

It was dreadful to be alone in a storm. But it was even more dreadful when it happened at Christmastime. Emily wept until she could weep no more.

———

Emily was grateful that Sophie had heard of her Christmas plight and invited her to share simple celebrations with her and her little family.

It helped to ease her pain at not being with her own family.

She even received a Christmas gift later in the day—one that brought tears to her eyes.

She had left Sophie's early so that she might add wood to her fire, and had just removed her coat when there was a knock on her door. To Emily's surprise, Timmie and Rena stood there when she answered the rap.

"Come in," Emily invited, fear gripping her heart. *Is there trouble at home again?* she wondered, but the children did not appear frightened.

"We came to say Merry Christmas," said Rena as she moved into the warmth of the kitchen, a gleam in her eye.

"Why, thank you," began Emily, but Timmie could not hold back his excitement.

"We brought you something," he declared, his eyes mirroring the glow in Rena's.

Emily looked at their empty hands, puzzled.

Timmie was fiddling with coat buttons, and Emily noticed that he wore no mittens. Then he reached inside his jacket and withdrew a black and white kitten with green-flecked eyes and a pert pink nose. Around its neck a worn hair bow had been carefully tied.

"They are big enough now," explained Timmie with a grin.

"This is the prettiest one," added Rena, one hand gently stroking the soft fur of the tiny animal.

"It's beautiful," agreed Emily, the tears forming in her eyes, and she reached out for the kitten that Timmie held toward her.

For a moment she could not speak. Her eyes brimmed and her throat constricted. *They have come through the drifts of snow to bring me a Christmas kitten. A real gift of love—from my own needy, caring Magi.* Emily fought hard for control.

"Is it a boy or a girl?" she asked when she could trust herself to speak.

"A boy," answered Timmie. "Mama said a girl might be a bother. You'd not know what to do with all the babies."

Emily smiled at the candid appraisal.

"Does he have a name?" she asked, stroking the kitten's back and being thanked with a soft purr.

Rena bobbed her head vigorously. "I named him," she informed Emily, "but you can call him whatever you want. He won't mind."

"What did you call him?" Emily asked.

"Walter," said Rena.

Emily wondered if she managed to hide her surprise. Walter seemed a strange name for a kitten.

"Well, if his name is Walter, we'll call him Walter," she said with finality.

Rena beamed.

"Now," suggested Emily, "let's allow Walter to explore his new home while I get you some hot chocolate."

Then Emily grabbed her coat. "You wait here," she told the youngsters. "I'll be right back."

Never had Emily borrowed from neighbors before, but now she hastened to Sophie's. She could not let the children start out for home in the cold without warming up their small bodies.

———

The winter was a difficult one for Emily. Often she went to bed with little in her stomach. Her cupboard was seldom supplied with the items she really needed to give her proper nourishment. And now she had to share her milk with Walter as well. She wondered that she was not sick more. All around her, colds and flu kept her parishioners in bed. And whenever possible, Emily called on those who were ill, offering what little help and encouragement she was able. She did suffer from a cold on two occasions and a flu sent her to bed for two days, but for the most part, she managed to keep going.

Severe illnesses kept Dr. Andrew busy day and night for a

number of weeks in February. He looked haggard and weary when Emily met him on the street.

Then word came that old Mr. Woodrow had passed away. He was from a family Emily did not know well. She had called there on two occasions but had received a very cool reception. She immediately recognized an opportunity to reach out to the elderly widow.

It was a miserable drive out to the Woodrow farm. The long winter that had piled high drifts of snow was gradually giving way to the mud of early spring. Emily urged her team through the ruts and mud holes, coaxing them to quicken their pace even though the buggy wheels clogged with the heavy gumbo.

At the farm home she found the new widow alone. Mrs. Woodrow had no family to share her mourning, and it seemed that the neighbors either had not yet heard the news or else did not know quite how to respond.

The woman's eyes did not soften as she saw Emily, but she did nod her head for Emily to enter as she held the door.

"I'm so sorry about the—the . . ." Emily did not know how to choose her words. She had heard that the couple had done nothing but quarrel for the past twenty years. "The death of your husband," Emily finished lamely.

Mrs. Woodrow just nodded again.

"I came to see if there is anything I can do."

The woman pushed some papers off a chair, letting them fall to the floor in disarray, and indicated that Emily could sit down.

Emily removed her mud-spattered coat and, without invitation, hung it on a crowded hook on the wall and took the offered chair.

After waiting for what she considered a suitable time, Emily cleared her throat. "Do you need any help with—the—the arrangements?" she asked softly.

"You bury?" asked the woman bluntly.

The words surprised Emily. "Well, no—I have never—never conducted a funeral service," she stammered, but quickly added as she saw the woman's expression, "but I'm sure that Rev.

Witt—our district superintendent—would come or send another minister."

The woman looked relieved.

"We need a coffin," the woman said.

"Would you like me to have one sent out from town?" Emily asked.

Mrs. Woodrow nodded.

"When would you like the funeral?" Emily continued.

"The quicker, the better," the woman responded without hesitation.

"I'll see how quickly I can get someone," Emily promised, and Mrs. Woodrow seemed satisfied with that.

"Where is the—the deceased?" Emily asked in a hesitant voice.

"In the back room," the woman said with a nod of her head. "I been sleepin' here on the floor."

Emily looked around her. *The body is right here in this house!* She shivered, then turned her attention to the blankets lying in a heap by the kitchen stove.

Emily rose. "Is there anything else I can do before I go?" she asked. The woman stood and moved toward the aforementioned back room. Without a word to Emily, Mrs. Woodrow opened the door, entered the room, and Emily could hear her moving about.

Soon she was back, a worn, threadbare black suit and a white shirt in her arms.

"Here's his buryin' things," she said to Emily. "Guess he should be washed and shaved."

Emily stared blankly at the woman. The woman was placing the items in Emily's hands and Emily took them dumbly, the truth slowly sinking in. *She expects me to prepare the body for burial.* Emily swallowed and tried to speak but the words would not come.

"There's water in the teakettle, and the basin is there on the corner stand. His razor is on that shelf."

Woodenly, Emily moved forward. She poured water into the basin, gathered together the shaving tools and lifted the much-used towel from the peg. Then, her arms laden, she moved toward the back room.

It was cold in the room. A strange odor seemed to fill the place. Enough light came from the small window to outline the still form on the bed. His eyes were fixed in a blank stare at the ceiling above his head and his mouth, empty of most of his teeth, hung open. Emily shuddered and wanted to run. She had never touched a dead body before, let alone prepared one for burial. She had no idea what was to be done.

She closed her eyes and another shudder ran through her. "I can't do this," she whispered. "I can't."

But a new thought flashed into her mind. *This might be the only bridge to reaching the woman out there.*

Emily steeled herself and set down her basin. She laid the clothes carefully on the bed and prepared herself for the ordeal ahead.

"Dear God, help me," she prayed. "I need your help in a way I've never needed it before," and Emily reached out a shaking hand to touch the arm of the man who lay on the bed.

It was stiff and cold to her tentative touch. A shiver went all through her, but she straightened her shoulders, pressed her lips tightly together and began the unwanted task.

———

Rev. Witt was not available, so Fred Russell was sent in answer to Emily's plea. Emily was disappointed that Agatha did not accompany him, but their baby was due any day.

Emily was relieved to see Fred and to turn the situation over to someone who had some experience in handling it.

Mrs. Woodrow wanted no church service.

"I just want him buried," she insisted in a hard voice, and Emily was glad that it was Fred who would be supervising the arrangements.

The neighborhood men prepared the grave. A number stood silently while the coffin was lowered and a few words from Scripture were spoken. Emily felt rather empty inside, as if something important wasn't quite finished.

As the small crowd drifted away, Emily thought she should invite Fred for supper but didn't know what she could serve him. He solved her dilemma by excusing himself. He was anxious to get back home to Agatha, and Emily nodded understand-ingly.

As she watched him go, she was glad the day was over. Mr. Woodrow's widow had already gotten a ride home from a neigh-bor. Emily walked from the cemetery, down the road toward the little town.

She felt discouraged as she trudged along. Mrs. Woodrow had not so much as muttered a "thank you" to anyone who had been involved in helping her.

Emily passed the post office and decided to check for mail. She didn't get much, but occasionally a letter came from home or from one of her Bible school friends. Emily would welcome such a letter now.

There were two pieces of mail that awaited her. One was a letter from the district superintendent with news of the coming conference. Emily was excited to learn that she would be ex-pected to be there. She would see many of her old friends again. *That's almost as good as going home!* she exulted.

The second letter puzzled her as she looked at the bold script and reread the return address. *It's a letter from Ross Norris. Imagine that! Ross, of all people! Why would he be writing me?* Emily had been interested in him when they were in Bible school, but she was sure they hadn't said more than a dozen words to each other during the whole time. Ruth wrote that Olive had broken her engagement to Ross, Emily remembered. Excitedly she held the envelope, but she resisted the urge to open it immediately and made herself wait until she was in the privacy of the parsonage. But that resolve did not stop the ques-tions from chasing through her mind.

Chapter Twenty-one

Conference

Ross's letter was full of newsy bits concerning their Bible school classmates. It was open and friendly, but Emily found herself still puzzling as she read. *Why has he written—to me? He's never done so in the past. Perhaps I'm trying to read more into it than I should. Why should it be so strange for a man to think of a former classmate and drop her a friendly note?* Emily assured herself that the letter was nothing more than that.

But an odd little feeling still tugged at the corners of her mind—especially when she read the last paragraph.

I have been doing some serious thinking recently. I saw Lacey at a youth meeting. He's really changed a lot since our Bible school days. He is so excited and happy about the chance to be in the ministry that I began to wonder if I had missed something important. I am even giving some consideration to entering the ministry myself.

Emily felt excitement course through her. *A minister? Ross? How wonderful if—* But Emily quickly checked herself and carefully folded the letter. She turned her attention instead to the other letter and the information on the coming conference, welcoming a change and a time for some spiritual refreshment.

Emily would take the train to Regis for the conference. On the day of the departure she was up early, took Walter to Sophie's to be cared for by the children, checked and rechecked her packed valise and tried desperately to get her unruly hair neatly tucked beneath her deaconess bonnet.

"Be sure to wear your deaconess badge," Mrs. Witt had instructed all the girls at their orientation meeting. "It lets the public know you are a member of the ministry."

Emily took her button from her handkerchief box and pinned it securely to the lapel of her coat. It wouldn't do to lose it.

She was at the train station much earlier than necessary, but she was too excited and nervous to stay at home. Nicky and Johnnie came by on some errand for Sophie and couldn't resist stopping to chat.

"We're gonna have fun with Walter."

"Are ya takin' the train?"

"How far are ya goin'?"

"When will ya come back?"

"Have ya ever been on a train before?"

"How do ya know when to get off?"

Their questions flowed thick and fast and Emily could not get one answered before the next one came at her. But their chatter did help the wait to pass more quickly.

Emily had another visitor at the train station. Mr. Travis came by, walking a fairly straight line. He had even made an attempt to comb his hair. He gave her a gap-toothed grin. His clothes were still hanging on a frail body and his chin was raggedly shaven, but he did tip his hat and bid her a good morning.

Emily knew he wanted to chat, but she felt herself becoming at once angry and frightened. A man who would beat his wife and children might do anything. Emily did not encourage a conversation.

At length he turned and made his uneven way toward the downtown. Emily was relieved to see him go.

Then a thought flashed through her mind. *Christ died for him, too, you know.* Emily's cheeks grew hot as she thought about her distant treatment of him.

I'm sorry, Lord, she prayed. *You love Mr. Travis—help me to love him with your love.* Emily spent the rest of the time on the station platform praying for the whole Travis family. *And poor little Claude. Such a child to be off on his own. I wonder . . . I wonder where he is and if he is okay,* she thought as she prayed for him too.

Emily jerked to attention as she heard the whistle of the train. The out-dated passenger car was not a fancy one, but Emily sighed with relief as she settled her valise under the worn seat. With a bit of a jerk they were on their way. Emily looked out to see the familiar sights of her little town slip by. *I'm a real deaconess, and I'm on my way to the conference,* she let herself exult.

As they passed through the countryside, Emily recognized many of the farms she had visited. One was the farm of Mrs. Woodrow, and a chill went through Emily again as she thought of her experience preparing a body for burial.

"Well, it didn't kill me," she mused. "I'm still here—and well. But I certainly wouldn't want to repeat the ordeal. I'm sure Ruth will laugh when she hears about the squeamish Emily," and Emily smiled in spite of herself. It would be so much fun to have a good talk with Ruth again.

The blue-uniformed conductor came through the passenger car calling out "Tickets! Tickets!"

Emily fidgeted with her empty purse. She did hope she wouldn't have any explaining to do.

But when the conductor reached her, he looked squarely at her deaconess button, tipped his cap, smiled and said, "Good morning, ma'am. Have a good trip," then passed on to the next passenger. Emily breathed a sigh of relief and settled back into the worn plush of the seat.

Emily decided to pay particular attention to each town they came to so she wouldn't lose track of where they were. When Emily had traveled the train to and from Bible school, she had not had to pass through other towns but had always climbed down from the passenger car at the first stop. It would not do for her to miss her departure at Regis. But before they reached the first town, the conductor came through again.

"Swifton! Swifton!" he called loudly. "All out for Swifton."

Emily audibly sighed her relief. If he did that with each stop she would not need to worry about missing her own station. She leaned back against the seat and tried to enjoy the ride.

What if, for some reason, he does not call Regis? Emily thought. *I'd better be keeping track, just in case.*

But the conductor did not forget Emily's station. In fact, when he came through he looked directly at Emily as he called out Regis. Then he stopped at her seat and smiled again.

"Getting off here, ma'am?" he asked her, and Emily nodded, wondering how he knew.

"We bring a number of folks to conference every year," he explained. He reached for her valise and cautioned her gently, "Just stay in your seat until the train fully stops. Sometimes the train jerks a bit."

Emily nodded her thank you and waited for the jerk. The conductor then led the way down the narrow aisle, took Emily's arm for the dismount down the iron steps, and handed her the valise.

"Have a good conference," he bade her with another smile and a doff of his cap and then he was gone again.

"Emily!"

Emily wheeled to meet Ruth in a warm embrace.

––––––––––

The next two days were spent in meetings. Emily loved singing hymns of praise with the fellow worshipers. She thirstily drank in the messages that were given. She felt excitement to think she actually had a vote in the decisions of the church; and at mealtime or after the sessions were over for the day, she eagerly visited with old school friends and new acquaintances. Mostly the talk was about the ministries in which they were involved. Some brought glowing reports, others, like Emily, faced difficulty and challenge in trying to get a little work started.

But the time after the evening services belonged to Emily and Ruth, and instead of getting much-needed sleep, they often talked well into the night hours in the darkness of their shared room.

Ruth was still excited about being able to preach. "If only I didn't have to go calling," she told Emily candidly, "I would just love the work."

"Calling? That's the part I like most," Emily said in amazement.

"Oh-h, I dread it. I put it off—and put it off for as long as I can. I would much sooner be pouring myself into my next sermon."

Emily began to laugh softly. "We should be a team," she decided. "I would do the calling and you could do the preaching."

Ruth joined in her laughter.

"I do have some problems, though," confided Emily. "One in particular that really troubles me. One of my parishioners has a drunkard for a husband. When he drinks, which is often from what I can gather, he beats her. He would likely beat the children, too, if he could catch them, but they usually run and hide and the mother takes the brunt of his fury. It just sickens me. I don't know what to do."

Ruth sympathized but had little advice to offer. "Why don't you ask Rev. Witt?" she said at last. "He might know of some way to deal with it."

Emily decided to talk with him at the first opportunity.

Then the conversation changed direction.

"Do you have a . . . a friend?" asked Ruth hesitantly.

"Well, I guess Sophie is my best friend, even though—"

But Ruth's chuckle stopped Emily.

"I meant a male friend," she informed Emily.

Emily blushed and was glad for the darkness that hid her embarrassment. Immediately her thoughts flew to Shad. But she had not heard from him for months.

"No," she answered in the darkness.

There was silence for several minutes. Then Ruth spoke softly into the night and even though her voice was low, Emily could sense the excitement in it.

"I do."

"You do? Oh, Ruth!" squealed Emily and had to be shushed by her old roommate.

"You'll awaken everyone in the dorm," cautioned Ruth.

"Tell me about him," pleaded Emily. It was almost unbelievable that Ruth—Ruth who never seemed to care about fellows, who seemed oblivious to their existence—was actually confessing to being interested in one.

"Well," said Ruth and the tone of her voice betrayed her, "he is a farmer. He comes to all the services—been a wonderful help to me. He's taller than I am by about three inches, has dark hair and really pretty eyes. At least I think so."

Emily squealed again but quickly pulled a blanket up around her face to muffle the sound. "Are you getting married?" she asked her old roommate.

Ruth hesitated. "I still want to preach," she replied at last.

"Doesn't—doesn't he want you to?"

"He—he says it's fine with him, but . . . Well, it's hard work directing a church. I don't know if I could be both a wife and a—a pastor. And if I wasn't a good wife, I'd feel guilty. And if I didn't preach, I would feel cheated. And if we had children—then I'd really have a hard time trying to do it all."

Emily understood Ruth's dilemma.

Again there was silence. Emily spoke softly. "You are really going to have to pray this one through."

"I've prayed and prayed," admitted Ruth, "and I still don't know what to do."

"I'll pray with you," promised Emily and inwardly added Ruth's situation to her prayer list.

Emily did talk with Rev. Witt about the Travis family.

"This is a really tough situation," he said sadly. "One must move cautiously. Has she ever indicated that she needs or wants help?"

"No," admitted Emily, shaking her head.

"Are the children frequently abused as well?"

"They usually run away and hide," Emily answered, "but emotionally, I know they are damaged. I felt little Rena shiver with fear when I held her."

"One could report him to the authorities—but then, Mrs. Travis could do that herself."

"I—I honestly think she still loves him in some strange way. She doesn't want interference, but I just can't stand by and see—" Emily stopped for a moment and then continued. "She speaks of him as 'being sick.'"

The minister nodded again. "And so he is," he agreed, "very sick—in body and soul." He was quiet for a while, then looking up, he said, "It puts the church in a most difficult situation. We do not wish to break up families, but to allow a woman and her children to continue to suffer at the hands of such a man—that is unthinkable."

Emily nodded, sorrow shadowing her eyes.

"Offer the woman and her children all the love and support you can," the kind man went on. "And watch for an opportunity to talk with her frankly about her situation. Maybe from that discussion, something will become clear to you and to her. And keep praying for a change of heart in this man. The next time I visit you, I will look further into the matter."

He placed a fatherly hand on Emily's shoulder. "I know this is difficult," he said sympathetically. "We'll all be praying that God will give you wisdom beyond your years or experience."

Emily thanked him and, with tears threatening to spill over, excused herself.

"Emily! How are you?"

At the sound of the voice and the light touch on her arm, Emily whirled to meet Ross. She hadn't expected him to show up at the conference.

"Ross! What a surprise," she managed as she extended her hand.

Ross grinned. "I had to see all my old school friends," he said easily.

"Well, the last session dismissed about a half hour ago. Some of the people already left," Emily told him. But there was no disappointment on Ross's face.

"Well, you're still here," he countered and laughed at Emily's surprise.

"My train doesn't leave until morning," she explained. "I'll stay in the dorm another night."

"Good," he responded. "Then how about a meal with me at the Royale tonight?"

Emily was surprised. How many were the times she had longed for such an invitation? She stammered now, "That—that sounds like—a wonderful idea."

"Good! I'll pick you up around six then. We'll do all our catching up over a Chinese dinner."

Emily nodded dumbly. She couldn't believe this was actually happening.

Emily wanted her hair and her dress to be just right, and prepared carefully for her evening out. She actually had a date with Ross, something she used to dream about. She smiled as she worked at her hair nervously.

Just before leaving, she automatically reached for her black bonnet and then laughed at herself. *I certainly don't need that tonight!* she decided. And Emily carefully laid the bonnet back on the dresser.

Ross was prompt. He offered his arm and Emily took it shyly.

"You have a car?" she asked as he led her to the waiting automobile.

"Of course. I'm a man of great wealth now," he teased and they chuckled together.

"Well, I'm not," admitted Emily. "I still use a poky old team and buggy. But then, an automobile would never make it through Wesson Creek's mud holes anyway."

They laughed again.

"You really drive horses—through mud?" asked Ross seriously.

"I do. Some of the women still have to walk when they make their calls. I am blessed with transportation—thanks to my father," admitted Emily.

"You shouldn't have to do that," Ross argued firmly. "The men should be out there preaching."

"But there aren't enough men called," Emily countered. "Or, if they are—they aren't answering," she added slowly.

"Well, let's not talk about work tonight." Ross changed the subject smoothly. "Let's have a night of fun—and fellowship—as we used to say at school."

Emily laughed. She was ready for a night of fun and fellowship. It had been a long time since she had enjoyed the company of someone her own age.

Chapter Twenty-two

Back to Work

Emily had been back at her small parsonage for only six days when another letter came from Ross.

I had a delightful time the evening we went out for Chinese food, he wrote. *It made me realize that we have so much in common. I do wish I would have discovered it earlier. It was a shame to have wasted those two years at school.*

Emily frowned. Her two years at school had certainly not been wasted.

I was wondering when you might be this way again, Ross continued. *I really would like to see you. Until then, I guess I will just have to be content with writing—but a letter leaves so much to be desired.*

"Oh, my!" breathed Emily. "Exactly what is Ross trying to say?" she wondered.

Then Ross's letter told about his work managing a hardware store and his family and the town where he lived.

The man who owns the store lives in the next town and he says he may even sell it to me someday, Ross enthused on paper.

Emily frowned slightly. It seemed that Ross had forgotten about his possible call to the ministry. He appeared to be making future plans with no thought of that call.

Emily decided she needed a diversion—a busy diversion—and deemed it a good day to get to work on her small garden plot. She hoped she would not need to go through another win-

179

ter on such scanty fare. Mrs. Witt had thoughtfully provided each of the young deaconesses with seeds from her own garden. Emily reached for them now and sorted the seeds out on her kitchen table. Then she slipped into her rubber overshoes and went out to check her backyard. It was much too wet for digging. Keenly disappointed, Emily decided to go visit Sophie instead.

Sophie was pleased to see her.

"Sit down," she said. "I'll get us some coffee."

Sophie brought two cups to the table and lit a cigarette. "So how was yer trip?" she asked with interest.

"Great," answered Emily and felt her face flush. Why was Ross the first thought she had in connection with her trip?

"Good," responded Sophie. Then added rather listlessly, "Things ain't been all thet great here."

"Why, what's wrong?" asked Emily with concern.

"It's Nicky. He's been sick. At first I thought it was jest some little bug—but he didn't get no better, so I called Doc yesterday. He don't know what's the matter either."

An unnamed fear twisted a knot in Emily's stomach. "It isn't serious, is it?"

"Don't know. I hope not. But Doc says he don't even know what medicine to give."

Sophie's expression gave away her worry.

"Oh, Sophie," said Emily softly, "we need to pray."

Tears ran down Sophie's cheeks. Emily reached for her hand and bowed her head, "Dear God," she began, "you know all about Nicky and his need. We don't know what is wrong. Even the doctor doesn't know yet what is wrong. Give the doctor wisdom as he seeks for the right medicine, and help Nicky to be better soon. And be with Sophie. It hurts to see a child ill, Lord. Help her to trust you and to be able to rest at night. Thank you, Lord, for all you do on our behalf. Amen."

Emily lifted her eyes. Sophie was still crying softly, but there was a crooked smile playing about her lips. The ash of the cigarette grew longer and longer, some of it spilling onto the table top.

"Thanks," muttered Sophie. "I was about beside myself. Thanks. It's such a relief. It's been worryin' me sick."

Emily was a bit surprised. She gathered from Sophie's simple words that she considered her son as good as well. Perhaps Sophie's faith was stronger than hers. Emily felt a bit of shame. She also felt some fear. She had known the Lord long enough to realize that God's answers sometimes did not come quite as one had asked.

"May I see Nicky?" Emily asked hesitantly.

Sophie smiled. "Sure," she said. "You can take him some of this chicken soup. I made it especially for him, but he ain't been able to eat a bit. He's likely half starved now." And Sophie busied herself with preparing food for her son.

But Emily found a very ill Nicky. His face was flushed a deep pink, his eyes were bright with fever. He moaned as he tossed restlessly on his pillow. Emily sat beside him and bathed his face from the basin on the stand beside him. She tried to coax some of the broth into him, but he could not swallow. Emily now became fervent in her praying.

"Oh, God," she pleaded, "I didn't know how sick he is. Please, dear Lord, we need your help. Nicky needs your help. He's lost weight. He's so sick. Help the doctor. Show him what to do. Touch Nicky's little body, Lord. We need you. Please, God."

Emily stayed all day with Nicky. Sophie, looking puzzled, came and went as her customers allowed. Emily had prayed. Why was it taking so long?

Emily did not go home even that night, except to care for Walter and then slip back. "You try to get some sleep," she urged Sophie, but Sophie paced the room restlessly until Dr. Andrew made a late call and left two tablets that would allow Sophie to rest.

The next day Sophie attached a sign on the cafe informing customers that she would not be opening, left her door locked and her blinds down, and stayed the day with Nicky.

Emily was concerned about the other three children. They too lived with fear. Emily did not know whether to offer to take them to her house and thus leave Sophie alone, or to stay with Sophie and leave the frightened children exposed to the anguish of the illness.

Again that night, Emily stayed with the family. Around one o'clock she slipped into her coat and let herself out the door. Nicky was worse. They needed Dr. Andrew.

Nicky died at quarter to three. There was nothing any of them could do to save him. Emily reached for Sophie to give all the support she could, but Sophie stepped back and pushed Emily's hands away.

"No!" she hissed. "No! No, ya prayed. Ya asked God. Why? Why did He let it happen? How could He? How could He? I was the one who was bad—not my Nicky." Sophie threw herself on the bed and gathered her son into her arms.

"Leave her," Dr. Andrew said softly to Emily. "She must express her grief in her own way. You go home now."

Emily went, dragging her tired body and her confused mind. Over and over her own thoughts echoed those of Sophie. *Why? Why did it happen this way? Why didn't you heal him, Lord? You could have. You could have.*

Emily's faith had never been so shaken. She sobbed long after she should have been asleep, and when she finally did drift off she was totally spent emotionally. *Will I ever be able to reach out to Sophie again? Will she ever let me?*

———

The funeral was held on a sunny spring afternoon. Rev. Witt came for the service. Sophie sat stoically in the small church, holding her three children close to her. Her eyes were sunken and red-rimmed, but she did not weep at the funeral.

Emily wept, sobs shaking her slight frame.

"Oh, Nicky," she cried, "you were such a sweet child. We are going to miss you terribly. And Sophie. The pain of Sophie. I can't imagine the pain!"

After the graveside ceremony was over, Sophie placed a small pink rose on the coffin of her son and turned to go back to the cafe.

Emily wanted to speak to her, but the retreating back was straight, stiff, and the head held defiantly high.

I'll slip over later, Emily promised herself and turned to invite the Witts to the parsonage for tea.

———

Emily visited Sophie three days later. The woman welcomed her cordially enough, but the coldness did not leave her eyes.

They sat at the corner table, their coffee cups before them, each with her own thoughts.

Emily wished to offer some words of hope, but she didn't know how to express them. Silently she prayed for wisdom—for guidance.

"I . . . I would love to have the children stay for dinner after church on Sunday," Emily began slowly.

Sophie's eyes lifted then. Emily could see the hardness there.

"They won't be in church on Sunday," she replied sharply.

Emily's eyes showed no surprise, but she asked softly, "Will you be—be away?"

"No. No, we'll be right here. They'll jest not be goin' anymore, thet's all."

"Oh, Sophie," breathed Emily before she could stop herself.

"Look, Emily," Sophie said frankly. "I don't mind callin' you a friend. Ya stayed with me and Nicky night an' day when he was sick, but don't—don't ever try to shove yer religion on me again—understand?"

Emily looked into the cold, dark, angry eyes.

"As I see it, either He couldn't do anythin' to save my son—or He wouldn't. Either way, He's not the kind a God I want or need."

"Oh, He could have—" began Emily.

"Then why *didn't* He?" spat Sophie, and she rose quickly from the table, her eyes flashing.

"I—I don't know," replied Emily helplessly. "I just don't know."

"Then don't do yer preachin' in here—to me or to my children—ever again!" snapped Sophie, and she turned her back and walked briskly to her counter.

Emily arose and slowly left the small cafe, her shoulders drooped and her eyes brimmed with tears. "I don't know," she wept softly. "I really don't know."

Emily, numb with sorrow, hardly was aware of what she was doing the rest of the morning. But that afternoon Mrs. Woodrow surprised her at her door. Emily welcomed her warmly and hurriedly set teacups and a small plate of cookies on the table.

"I didn't come to sip and chat," the woman said gruffly. "I came to find out how to get ready to die."

Emily did not know exactly what the woman meant. "You mean you—you want to arrange for your funeral service?" she inquired.

"Lands no!" exclaimed the woman. "I don't care none if they throw my body in the lake. I need to be ready to die."

Emily understood then, but she could not have been more surprised. "I see," she said slowly, feeling the enormous weight of the responsibility that was hers. She lifted her Bible from the shelf and began to turn the pages. She knew all the appropriate scriptures. She had carefully trained for this moment during her Bible school preparation. *Please make the truth come alive to Mrs. Woodrow,* she prayed as she came to the book of Romans.

"The Bible says that *all* have sinned," began Emily, pointing to the scripture passage.

"I know that," responded the woman. "I've lived long enough to see it for myself."

"And the wages of sin—is death," Emily went on.

Mrs. Woodrow nodded. Emily could see that she accepted that as fair.

"But God loved us and sent His Son to take the death penalty in our place. We are talking now about spiritual death—separation from God and punishment for our sins. We all still die physically."

The woman nodded again, and Emily sensed her impatience.

"What I need to know is how to get that forgiveness," she prompted Emily.

"Well, God's forgiveness is a gift. We need to accept the gift by accepting God's Son. We repent of our sins and we receive His forgiveness in Jesus' name. He will help us turn from what we have been to what He wants us to be. God gives us a cleansed heart. We accept, with gratitude, His salvation. And then we are baptized to show others that we are now members of the believing church."

Emily swallowed quickly. She wasn't sure if she had explained it clearly or if the woman could understand the concept of salvation through faith.

But Mrs. Woodrow nodded again. "And how do you do that?" she asked.

"Is that what you wish?" asked Emily.

"That's what I came for," responded the woman.

Emily flushed. "Well then, you pray. You pray and ask God—and He will do the rest."

"I don't know how to pray," stated the woman. "That's why I came to you."

"Let's pray," invited Emily. "You may repeat after me—if you mean the things I'm saying." And Emily led the woman in a brief prayer of request for God's forgiveness and salvation.

At the end of the prayer Mrs. Woodrow's face had relaxed. Her eyes, formerly so troubled, were shining now.

"When do I get baptized?" she asked simply.

"Well I—I need to make arrangements with Rev. Witt. I don't do the baptizing myself. He will come—"

"Well, just don't wait too long," cautioned the woman. "I could die most any time."

Emily denied the smile that tugged at her lips. Instead she spoke evenly, slowly. "You will want to have fellowship with God, now that you are in His family," she said simply. "We do that through reading His Word, the Bible, and through prayer."

"I can read," she answered, "but I can't pray."

"All you do is talk to your Father—much as you are talking to me now. But it doesn't even need to be out loud. Just open up your heart to Him. Any time. Any place. Whenever you feel you wish to talk to Him. And share your—your troubles. Your hurts. Your joys. Anything. And ask Him to help you to understand more about Him each day."

"Do I have to come to church?" asked the woman, and Emily did smile then.

"You don't *have* to come to church," she said, "but I would encourage you to come. There you can grow as you hear God's Word and fellowship with other Christians. It's very helpful to come to God's house as often as you can."

Mrs. Woodrow nodded.

"Do you have a Bible?" asked Emily.

"My husband's ma gave him one when he was a boy. It's still there."

"Good," said Emily.

The woman's eyes suddenly filled with tears. "I wish he would have read it—believed it," she said softly. "Might have made a heap a difference." Then she quickly added, "But I can't blame him none for the way I been. I had enough smarts to know I wasn't doin' right."

Emily nodded.

"I'd like that tea now," said the woman, sniffing, and she took off her hat that had seen many seasons and settled herself at Emily's table.

Chapter Twenty-three

Autumn Blues

Emily looked dismally at the patchy row of carrots, the few potato plants, the yellowish leaves of the one tomato plant, the skinny beets and the stunted corn in her garden. She would not have much to go on through the coming winter with such a skimpy crop. She heaved a sigh and thanked God for Mrs. Reilly's hens. At least she would have eggs to eat.

"I had so hoped . . ." she mused wishfully, then turned her back on the garden patch.

"Well, at least there are a few meals there," she said to herself as she went back inside to prepare for another day of visiting the families in her community.

During four days of rain, Emily had paced her small kitchen floor waiting for the sky to clear. Walter had chased along after her, playfully grabbing at her shoelaces. It was important to her to make another call on Mrs. Woodrow, who, as she wished, had been baptized by Rev. Witt and was coming to church faithfully. Emily marveled at the woman's hunger for the Word and the change in her over the past few months. In fact, everyone in the town had noticed the change in Mrs. Woodrow.

But word had come that the woman was ill. Emily took one more look at the gray skies and decided to hitch her team to the buggy, rain or not.

It was a mistake. The side road that led to the Woodrow farm was rutted and full of holes at the best of times, but with

187

the heavy rains that had fallen, it was next to impassable. Big
John had tried to warn Emily, but she quietly pushed aside his
gruff prediction and went ahead.

The first trouble came in the form of another heavy shower.
Emily gritted her teeth against the cold rain and kept her
horses headed in the direction of Mrs. Woodrow's farm.

When she turned off the main road onto the side road that
led to the farm, she discovered firsthand how accurate Big John
had been. The road to the Woodrow house was even worse than
she had feared. Deep, gummy mud holes bogged down her
buggy, and it was all her strong team could do to keep the small
wagon moving.

Emily lurched from one hole to another, trying to pick her
way through. To make matters worse, the rain running down
her face prevented her from seeing clearly. Much of the ground
was under a layer of water, and Emily hardly knew where to
aim the team next.

And then the inevitable happened. The buggy wheels ca-
reened into a particularly deep hole, and Emily heard the sick-
ening splinter of wood. She had broken a wheel. The horses
strained, trying to get the obstinate vehicle free from the cum-
bersome burden of mud, but Emily knew that to attempt to pull
the buggy out would only mean more damage to the wheel.

"Whoa-a," she called, pulling hard on the reins.

Emily looked dismally at the muddy road. Then she slipped
off her shoes and stockings, hoisted her skirts as far as her
dignity would allow, and climbed down over the muddy buggy
wheel.

She gasped at the depth of the hole and the cold ground as
she sank down in mud past her ankles. She could hardly move
one foot in front of the other. For several minutes she struggled
with the tugs, but they were wet and sloppy, and her hands
could not get a proper grip. In the meantime the horses shifted
impatiently, lifting one foot after the other with a strange suck-
ing sound. Working as quickly as she could, Emily finally freed
the team and managed to get them off to the side of the road
where she tied the horses to a tree.

"If I had a husband," Emily mumbled, "I would not need to
do this."

She padded back to the buggy, retrieved her shoes and stockings, and went on to the Woodrow farm on foot.

Mrs. Woodrow was not as sick as Emily had feared, and Emily was relieved to find her sitting before a warm fire, a cup of hot lemon juice before her and her Bible on her knees.

"My lands, girl, you'll catch your death!" the woman exclaimed when she saw Emily.

Emily only smiled. She had stopped long enough to wash her dirty feet in a cold puddle and slip back into her stockings and shoes. Still, she shivered as she entered the room.

"Sit down, sit down," the woman prompted. "Pull your chair right up there to the fire. Here, drink this. It'll warm you," she encouraged as she shoved a cup of hot lemon drink toward Emily.

After the visit, Emily again removed her shoes and stockings and went back to retrieve her team. She rode Shadow into town, and on to the Travis farm, leading Star behind her, her muddy, dripping skirts spread out over Shadow's broad back.

When the world finally stopped dripping, she had to send the blacksmith out for her buggy. She worried about the expense of the broken wheel, but he waved her money aside. "Seems I should be able to do some small thing for the church," he said, and Emily thanked him sincerely.

After a few days the sun came out in full strength, and the roads began to dry again. Emily had her buggy, solid and sound again, and her horses waiting for her at the Travis farm. Emily was ready to make up for lost time.

She began the rounds of familiar places, greeting people she had come to know. Most of them were glad to welcome her to their kitchen, but not many promised to visit her church in return, though a few did say they'd stop by for a cup of tea.

Emily was about to pass a vacant farmyard when she noticed a wagon in the yard. She took a closer look. Yes, two horses stood in the corral, and the fenced pasture beside the road held a few head of cattle.

With a quickened pulse, Emily turned her horses down the

lane. *Here's a new family,* she thought joyfully. *One on which I've never called before. Perhaps they'll be new members for our little congregation.*

A man in the yard was working on a stretch of broken fence. He lifted his head and looked her way. He seemed young— perhaps newly married and starting out on his own for the first time.

"Hello," greeted Emily. "I was just passing and noticed that this farm is now occupied. Welcome to the community."

"Thank you," he responded, and laid aside the hammer, touched his cap, and stepped closer to Emily's buggy. He had the brownest eyes she had ever seen.

Emily did not know what to say next. He solved the problem for her. "Are you the community welcoming committee?" he asked, teasing in his voice.

"Well, no," laughed Emily. "Actually, I am the—the worker at the little mission in town. I just stopped to give an invitation to our services. I'd love to meet your wife."

"I'd love to introduce you—only I don't have a wife . . . yet."

"I'm—I'm sorry," muttered Emily, embarrassed.

The man smiled. "No problem," he assured her. He went on. "Then there is a church here. Ma was afraid there might not be. She'll be pleased when she hears there is."

"Your mother attends church?" Emily inquired, thinking, *He must still live with his folks.*

"Regularly! And she tries to make sure that all her offspring do too."

Emily felt her heart quicken. *New members for our little church!* She handed the reins to the young man and moved to descend from the buggy. "I'd love to meet your mother," she said emphatically.

He put out a hand to help her down and led her horses to the hitching rail.

"That would be nice," he responded, his eyes sparkling just a bit. "I expect her next Sunday afternoon."

Emily could feel the color rising in her cheeks. "She isn't here?"

"No, ma'am," the young man answered with a shake of his head.

"She isn't moving in until Sunday?"

"I expect her on Sunday—but only to call. She lives in Meldon. I'm on my own now." He stopped long enough to lift the hat from his head, wipe a sleeve across his sweaty brow. "I'm just starting to farm my own place," he said, gazing out across the acres.

Emily looked at the tall, broad-shouldered young man with love-of-the-land clearly showing in his dark brown eyes. She hadn't a doubt that he'd make out just fine.

"Then I guess I should be on my way," she stated.

"I would be happy to bring some lemonade to the porch," he offered.

"That's very kind," replied Emily, "but I really think—"

"It's a warm day," insisted the young man. "I'm about ready for a break. And Mother always taught us to take care of God's servants." He smiled.

Emily returned the smile. "A glass of lemonade on the porch would be nice," she conceded, and fell into step with the young man.

Carl Morgan was in church every Sunday. He brought produce to her door. He volunteered to haul her wood, work on her skimpy garden, and build the fire in the church stove when needed.

Emily enjoyed the attention. She enjoyed his taking some of the burdens that she had carried for so long. But she did not enjoy the strange little warning that kept flashing through her mind.

Ruth's dilemma was a constant reminder. Ruth had written that she had let the young man go his own way. "I could not see how I could be wife, mother and minister," Ruth had written. "God has not yet released me from my call, and I know I could not turn my back on it."

But Emily argued that her situation might be different from Ruth's. Surely she could live right here in the community and still serve the church and be the wife of an area farmer.

Carl had not as yet asked her to be his wife. "He is considerate and manly and a sincere believer," Emily told herself. She was sure all she had to do was to encourage him and he would ask for her hand.

"This is ridiculous," she finally said aloud one evening. "You don't marry simply to have someone to harness the horses or haul the wood!"

From that time on, Emily carefully guarded her words and actions when she was around Carl. She, like Ruth, could not give up her calling until God released her, and He had not done so as yet.

When I marry—if I marry, Emily reminded herself, *it must be to someone who shares my commitment, not robs me of it.* From then on Emily busied herself even more with the task of outreach and nurture of the community.

But regardless of her new resolve, memories of another man, Shad Austin, began to return to her daytime thoughts and her nighttime dreams. *He seemed so comfortable to be with—so right,* thought Emily. *If only . . . if only . . .*

Then Emily's thoughts turned to Ross—Ross whose warm letters arrived each week. Now Emily felt more confused than ever.

———

A knock at her door brought Emily's attention from the Sunday sermon over which she was laboring. She was not expecting company. The women who shared neighborhood news with her over a cup of tea never came on Saturday, knowing it was the time she devoted to her Sunday preparations.

But when Emily opened the door, there stood Ross!

"Ross! What a surprise," Emily managed, and he moved to enter without invitation.

"I thought it was a nice day for a picnic," he answered cheerfully.

It was a glorious fall day. The leaves were delightful shades of reds and yellows. The sun hung lazily in the sky, and birds flitted here and there, calling their last farewells before departing for the south.

"A picnic? It *does* sound like fun."

"Then grab your coat—or whatever you need, and let's be off. I already have lunch in the car."

It was so tempting. "But I'm not ready for Sunday," Emily moaned.

"Sunday?"

"My sermon," Emily reminded him.

"Your sermon? Can't it wait?"

"I'm afraid not. It takes me most of Saturday to properly prepare it."

"But just this once, couldn't you cut short the time? Use an old one or something. No one would remember. Just change a few words."

Emily shook her head.

"You shouldn't be—" started Ross, but he stopped and changed his tone.

"Oh, Emily," he said, and moved closer to her, "I've traveled miles to see you. It is my only free day. I had a picnic lunch specially prepared. I was so looking forward to seeing you again." His hands on her waist, he pulled her closer to him and pressed his lips against her hair. "Please," he pleaded. "Please."

Emily pushed away slowly, not comfortable being held by a man to whom she had made no commitment. She lifted Ross's hands from her waist and stepped back to look at him.

"Ross," she began slowly, "I'm sorry. Truly I am. I enjoy your friendship, but I—my first commitment is to the Lord. And that includes preparation of a Sunday sermon, and I'm afraid—I'm *sure* that is what I must do."

She thought she saw anger in his eyes.

"You—you can't understand that, can you?" she dared to ask.

He shook his head stubbornly. "I thought a woman's place was in the home—as a wife, a mother," he retorted.

"I agree," she admitted, then added quickly, "unless God calls her into something else. Then she must be obedient to His call."

"Let the *men* preach," he countered. "You can't do the full work anyway. You can't marry or bury or baptize. You call that ministry?"

Emily forced herself to ignore his sarcasm. "If I had a husband who would preach, I would be glad to allow him that privilege," she returned firmly. "This community needs the Word of God. Until such time as a man comes to deliver it, the responsibility will be mine."

"Very well," he said in clipped tones. "I guess I will find someone else to share my picnic—and my future."

Emily sighed. "Yes," she replied evenly, "I guess you should."

Then he was gone, and Emily shed a few tears before she returned to her sermon.

"It's all right, Lord," she prayed. "I am quite prepared to serve alone—for as long as you need me."

Emily participated in the annual Autumn Picnic again. But without the presence of Shad, the day was not the same. She joined the Reillys at their table, but they made no comment about Shad missing the festivities for the first time—and Emily dared not ask. *In fact,* Emily thought, *Mrs. Reilly has not mentioned Shad for many months. Has there been some rift between them? He didn't even come visit this summer, as far as I know.*

Emily was puzzled, but her question went unanswered.

Chapter Twenty-four

Winter Wars

"I notice Sophie's kids don't go to yer Sunday school no more," Big John commented as Emily opened her purse to pay for her purchases.

"No, they don't," agreed Emily, sadness in her eyes. She had prayed so often that Sophie would relent after a time, but she was still adamant in her refusal to allow the children to return to church.

"Took it pretty hard, did she?" Big John continued.

How would you expect a mother to take it? Emily wanted to retort. Instead she made no reply.

"Thet's what I don't understand 'bout religion," John mused, almost to himself. "Ya say God loves. Ya say He is powerful. Ya say He can answer prayer. So how come ya didn't pray thet the boy would git better?"

"We did," said Emily honestly.

Big John looked at her triumphantly. "But He didn't answer, did He?"

"He answered," responded Emily evenly.

Big John looked surprised at her reply.

"The kid died!" he shot back at her.

"That doesn't mean God didn't answer our prayer," Emily answered softly, tears glistening in the corners of her eyes. "Oh, I know. He didn't answer in the way we wanted—the way we prayed. But we can't see the future. He can. He answered in the way He knew best."

"Humph!" Big John snorted. "Thet's the baloney ya religious people always spout. Don't make a lick of sense, an' ya know it. Either He ain't got the power to do what He promises, or else He don't care one little bit, thet's the truth o' the matter."

Emily straightened to her full height. "If I thought that for one minute," she said honestly, "I wouldn't be here."

"So why are ya here?" he challenged. "No man ask ya to wed?"

Emily gulped down her frustration. If he only knew the agony she had been through trying to weigh her desires to be a wife and mother against her call to the ministry. She blinked back tears and answered softly, firmly.

"Being here, as a single woman, is not easy. I do not relish the care of horses. I do not enjoy trying to produce a garden in a patch of weeds. I do not like hauling wood and water. I do not even enjoy the preparations of sermons—all 'manly' jobs, if you will. But God has called me here. I do not know why—nor do I ask. I only try to obey."

She picked up her small parcel. "And you can be assured," she went on, "I will be here—just as long as I feel this is where He wants me." She turned and quietly left the store.

She was annoyed with herself that she let Big John's barbs get to her. She would never, never be any witness to the man as long as she allowed him to trouble her so.

"Lord," she prayed, sitting at her little table stroking Walter's fur, "please help me to respond calmly to his honest questions and overlook the ones he asks simply to bother me. Help me to know what to say and how to say it. And help Big John to learn to love you."

———

Emily hurried the team home from her calling, feeling the sharp chill in the air. She let her horses through the pasture gate and moved quickly toward the Travis house. She was anxious to see how things had been going with the family. They had missed church on Sunday.

Mrs. Travis welcomed her warmly and insisted that she stop for a cup of hot chocolate. Two new bruises had appeared on the woman's forehead but she made no comment. They chatted lightheartedly over their cups.

"Mrs. Travis," Emily finally began carefully as she toyed with the teacup, "is there any way that I can help you?"

The woman looked surprised.

"I would be glad to make the call if you'd like your husband to get some—some medical help with his problem," Emily dared to continue.

Mrs. Travis looked alarmed and shook her head vigorously. "I don't want anyone butting into our family affairs," she said firmly. "We've made out fine till now. We'll make out fine in the future, too."

"But what about Claude?" Emily challenged.

"Had a letter from Claude," Mrs. Travis said proudly. "He's got him a job with a farmer over east of here. Plans on coming home for Christmas."

Emily was pleased to hear the news and said so to Mrs. Travis.

"But the other children?" pressed Emily. "What if Timmie and Rena decide to leave home at Claude's age? Will that be all right, too?"

Tears formed in the woman's eyes. She dropped her head and shook it sadly. "He's my husband," she whispered. "He's their father. It's just the drink that gets him—upset." Then she lowered her voice even further. "They might come and take him away if they know. I couldn't live with that. Do you understand? . . . No, I don't suppose you can."

"But they could help him," insisted Emily. "Bring him back again after he had conquered the problem."

"No. No—it doesn't work that way. He tried. He tried once before. He just came back worse."

Then she looked at Emily, the tears flowing down her cheeks. "Please, please," she pleaded, "leave things as they be. Please?"

Emily could only nod her head while despair filled her heart. What choice did she have? What else could she do?

Winter's snow fell in stinging crystals, biting at faces and uncovered hands. Strong winds swirled it round and round the little town, sculpting drifts in out-of-the-way places and sweeping white, glass-like particles against windowpanes and rooftops.

Emily was glad for a warm fire and plenty of wood, but she couldn't help worrying as she studied her little storage cupboard. Most of the few vegetables she had managed to draw from her little garden had now been eaten. And though the Sunday offerings had increased somewhat with the attendance of a few new members, it was still not enough to adequately cover her living expenses.

God will provide, she reminded herself.

By now she was out of flour and sugar—even the precious bit she kept for the guest's tea had been used. And she needed tea again as well. With the colder weather, more women were sure to be stopping for that cup of warmth and a chat when they came to town.

Emily folded her coat closely about her and hurried out into the driving snow. At the mercantile she carefully counted her coins as Big John waited on another customer. She simply did not have enough money for flour, butter, vanilla and sugar to make cookies.

She wondered what she should do. It wouldn't be very hospitable to serve just tea.

Emily's eyes scanned the shelves and bins and fell upon ginger snaps. Carefully she fingered her money again. She could do it.

When it was her turn, she ordered two dozen ginger snaps, one-half pound of sugar and a pound of tea. Then she counted out her money and left the store.

While Emily served her guests "store-bought" cookies, no one suspected she herself was living mostly on eggs scrambled, eggs fried, eggs boiled and eggs poached. Cream and butter came to the parsonage, along with an occasional frying chicken or small piece of beef, but Emily's diet varied little from day to day.

She tried hard to have at least one serving of vegetables daily, knowing that her body needed the nutrients, but at times it was as little as minced onion in her scrambled eggs.

Periodically, she counted out her coins and purchased another pound of cookies and another bit of sugar. If Big John wondered as he filled her orders, he didn't say anything.

———————

Emily had not seen Sophie for several weeks. Even after Sophie's conclusion that Nicky's death was God's fault, Emily had continued to visit the cafe for a cup of coffee and a little chat. But their times together became more strained, and Emily crossed the street less and less. She still prayed for Sophie and the children. She still worried and wondered about them, but she found the situation very awkward.

"If only she would let the children come," Emily often sighed. "They seem to miss it so much."

But Emily did not dare to approach Sophie again with her request.

One morning Emily went to the church earlier than usual. It was a cold, crisp Sunday, and she knew the stove would need extra time to heat the small building. Carl had stopped by the day before to tell her that he would not be able to be there. It was the first time Emily had to build her own fire for a number of Sundays.

She got the fire going, placed the few hymnals on the seats, arranged her teaching notes on the small podium, and then waited for the room to lose its chill and her congregation to arrive.

"There won't be many out this morning," she mused as she rubbed her hands together near the stove, trying to keep warm.

The door opened and Sophie pushed her head in. "May we come in?" she asked self-consciously.

Emily could not believe her eyes and ears. "Oh, Sophie!" she cried, hurrying to meet the woman.

Three beaming children bounded in ahead of their mother.

"We're comin' to church again!" exclaimed Olivia, clapping her small hands as she hopped her way across the floor.

"I'm so glad!" exclaimed Emily, and she knelt before the child and pulled her into her arms. "Oh, I have missed you," she said, a lump in her throat.

"We missed ya, too," said Olivia, wrapping her arms around Emily's neck.

Sophie was silent as she watched the exchange, but tears filled her eyes.

"It was the kids who made me see the truth," she explained to Emily, wiping her eyes.

Emily stood to her feet and took Sophie's hand.

"Last night when I was puttin' them to bed, Tommie said to me, 'Mom, do ya think Nicky's in heaven?' And I said of course I did. Then he said, 'But if we don't live the way Jesus wants us to, we won't be able to go there to see him.' An' he started to cry. 'I want to see Nick again, Mom,' he said. And I knew I wanted to see Nick again, too.

"But I didn't say so to Tommie. I jest couldn't let myself forgive God. An' then Johnnie spoke up. He said, 'Mom, do ya think that's why God let Nick die—so the rest of us would want to go to heaven?' " Sophie paused a moment to get control of her emotions.

"I couldn't answer thet question, but I thought about it long after the kids was asleep. Maybe that *is* why. I mean, if Nick had not died, I would've jest gone right on sendin' my kids to Sunday service, livin' my own life the way I want, never realizing thet I need God more'n any of 'em.

"God could've taken all my kids to heaven someday, an' I would've been left behind. I don't want thet, Emily. I want to go with 'em."

Sophie was crying hard now. Emily led her to a church pew and they knelt down together, and Emily carefully, tenderly led Sophie to understand and seek God's great forgiveness.

Emily was still feeling the thrill of Sophie's conversion the next morning when she went to get her two dozen cookies with the offering money. She even had a few extra cents with which to buy a handful of potatoes. God was so good. He had cared for Sophie. He was daily meeting Emily's needs. At least she had not gone hungry—and she again had enough change to buy cookies for her guests. Emily felt like singing as she entered the store.

"I see yer strays've returned," Big John said in a mocking voice, and Emily wondered if he had nothing better to do on Sundays than to sit and spy on her little flock.

Emily had a notion to ask him, but he continued, "Even Sophie herself."

"Yes," replied Emily, eyes shining. "Isn't God good?"

Big John just "humphed."

"I'm sorry—truly sorry that you are unable to accept the fact that there is a God—and that He loves us, and cares for us," Emily said boldly. She had never dared to talk to the man in such a straightforward fashion before. "Because He *is*. He exists—and He does care."

Big John cleared his throat.

"I've never said thet I don't believe there is a God—somewhere," he argued. "I jest don't think He's much in'erested in me," he countered.

"But He is," Emily responded. "Enough so that He sent His Son, Jesus Christ, to die for you. How much more could He care?"

"An' thet's another thing," Big John hurried to interrupt. "This Jesus bit. What makes ya think thet Jesus is God?"

"What do you mean?" Emily asked, stunned.

"Well, this here Jesus. He was a man—jest like me—or Walt or Jake. No different."

"No," countered Emily, shocked at his statement. "He was born to a woman—but He was God himself in a human body."

"And where do ya git thet stuff?" the man continued. "He died, didn't He? Can a God die?"

"*He* did," affirmed Emily. "He died—for us—because He *chose* to die. But He rose from the dead—by His own power. Can a mere man do that?"

"Nonsense!" snapped Big John. "Thet was a hoax. Men was bribed to say—"

"Then what about all of the people who saw Him after His death and resurrection?" asked Emily. "Is it logical that over five hundred witnesses could be wrong?"

But Big John did not answer her question. Instead he asked, "What makes ya think He's God?"

"The Bible confirms it," Emily replied firmly.

"Ya mean 'cause o' the Trinity?" snorted Big John.

"Yes. The Trinity."

"The word *Trinity* ain't even in the Bible," scoffed Big John.

"I know that," agreed Emily, looking directly into his eyes, "but the teaching is. Over and over it speaks of God the Father, of Christ His Son, of the Spirit that moves in the hearts of people. The concept of the Trinity is there, even though the word is not used."

"How can three people be one, answer me thet?" sneered Big John. "How can a person be spoken of as a son of God an' yet be God. How can ya be yer own son?"

"I don't know," Emily answered frankly. "I really don't know. I—I don't think that a human being can fully understand it. I don't think we have proper words to describe it. I think that God called Christ His Son because that relationship was something we *could* understand. There are no words in our human languages to describe the very special relationship of God the Father and God the Son."

"Pshaw!" exclaimed Big John. "Jest words to prove a belief ya can't support. When ya find reasons to believe all thet stuff ya teach—then maybe I'll listen to what ya got to say."

Emily was shaking.

"He was the son of God—not God," the man still insisted. "A 'little lower than the angels,' the Bible says. Don't tell me thet another man could do fer me what I ain't able to do fer myself. Trinity! Humbug!"

"I might not be able to explain it," Emily acknowledged humbly, "but I know that I believe it. With my whole heart I believe it."

"Yeah, an' men used to believe the earth was flat," Big John ridiculed.

Emily made herself smile and thanked him for her purchases as she left the store. There didn't seem to be any good reason to continue the argument.

"I do believe it," she said aloud as she trudged home through the snow. "I do—with all my heart."

But why? asked an inner voice. *Just because that's what you've been taught all your life?*

Though Emily would not have cared to admit it, her faith had been shaken by the exchange.

Chapter Twenty-five

The Answer

During the weeks that followed, Emily spent hours studying her Bible. *I must know for myself that Christ Jesus is God,* she decided. *It is essential to my teaching—to my whole life. If it is not so—then my faith—my devotion—is all in vain.*

As Emily studied, she took notes, slowly filling many pages. It was true, she discovered, that Scripture referred to Him over and over again as the Son. He himself made numerous references to the Father. *So,* thought Emily as she reviewed those scripture passages, *they are two distinct beings.*

She really never doubted that. Now Big John's next question haunted her. *How could He be the Son of God, and yet God himself?* Was He a created being, as some groups taught? Was He a lesser God, as others taught? How could one explain Christ as God without the concept of the Trinity?

Emily struggled on.

"What evidence do I have," she murmured, "that Christ is God?" and she dug more deeply into the pages of her Bible.

He does have power, she thought as she read the story of the healing of the lepers. But she quickly reminded herself that His followers were given power to heal as well. Hadn't Peter healed the lame man at the temple gate?

But Christ's power was different, she mused. With His own power He had raised himself from the dead. *A live man doesn't have such power,* Emily reasoned, *much less a dead one.*

It sounded like a solid argument.

But Emily needed more.

Again and again she found words like these: "I came from the Father and to Him I shall return." They were spoken from the lips of the Christ. He also stated, "If you have seen me, you have seen the Father." And He told His followers that He had existed from the beginning.

Then Emily began to discover some special evidence. Jesus Christ forgave sins. It was only God who could wipe man's sin from the record books.

Emily found too that the creation references interchanged God and Christ as the Creator.

But it was as Emily gathered the scriptures pertaining to the worship of God that her heart began to sing with joy.

Scripture was very specific. God would allow the worship of no other being than himself. He was a "jealous God." Man was to bow down to one God and one God only.

God's chosen people had learned that lesson through great tribulation and loss of land and even death. They had finally been broken from their idolatry under the rule of the Babylonians. God would not tolerate the worship of false gods.

Yet God allowed, yes, *demanded,* the worship of His Son, Jesus Christ. The religious leaders could not accept the position of Christ as God, and had rejected Him as an imposter.

"If they would have just understood the reality of the Trinity," Emily said to herself, "they could have accepted Christ and stayed true to the Father as well."

In the book written to the Philippians, Emily found the apostle Paul's statement: "At the name of Jesus every knee should bow, of things in heaven, and things in earth, and things under the earth; and that every tongue should confess that Jesus Christ is Lord, to the glory of God the Father."

Emily added page after page, as her notes grew, of accounts where Christ was worshiped, accepted worship, and was approved for worship by the Father.

"They have to be One!" cried Emily. "There is no other explanation. God would not share this honor with another, lesser, being."

It was enough for Emily. She still could not explain the Trinity. Three persons—yet One. But she was at peace in her own heart. Christ Jesus was not an imposter. He was not just a son of God. He was God himself. One in essence, one in Spirit—one with the Father in purpose and being.

Emily let the tears fall unchecked.

"My faith has been restored," she whispered to herself as she lovingly laid aside her Bible. Then she quickly added, "No, not restored. Strengthened."

———

After a great deal of thought and prayer, Emily approached Big John with her findings and some simplified notes. She handed them to him with an earnestness new to her.

"This is what I have discovered to support my beliefs," she said simply. "I do hope that you will study them. They are grounds for a living faith. Jesus Christ *is* God. The Trinity is a reality. I still can't explain it in human terms, but I know that God the Father, God the Son, and God the Holy Spirit do exist—as one."

The big man took her notes with no comment, then muttered something about the weather, his arthritis and his difficult sister. Emily felt it was all bluff. She smiled warmly at him, purchased her small bag of cookies and left the store.

———

Emily's cupboards now were truly bare. She had used the last of her eggs the night before. All she had left were a few cookies that she doled out carefully whenever she had guests, a few teaspoonfuls of sugar and enough tea for a skimpy pot.

"Lord, I don't know what to do," she confided. "I can't beg. But I don't think you want me to starve. I hate to do it, Lord, but I guess I'll have to visit somebody. I—I determined that I would never do my calling just to get a meal—but this time . . ."

Emily decided that though the day was cold, she would get her team and drive to the Reillys'. Not only would Mrs. Reilly welcome her and feed her well, but she would send her home with more eggs and milk as well. That would keep Emily going for several more days.

"Maybe I should even explain why I'm there," Emily told her conscience. She pulled on her heavy coat and tied a warm scarf snugly about her neck. After running a caressing hand over Walter's sleek fur, she checked her fire to make sure it was banked properly and walked to her door.

The thought of stepping out into the day made her shiver. She took a deep breath and pushed against the door. The frost had sealed the edges. Emily pushed harder and felt it give.

Her breath preceded her in silvery puffs of steam.

"It's too cold for man or beast," she said aloud, closing the door tightly behind her.

But as Emily turned to go, her foot kicked against something. Her first awful thought was of Mr. Travis. She had found him on her doorstep once before. If he were there now, he would be frozen stiff.

But it was not Mr. Travis. A small basket, bulging with contents and lightly dusted with snow over its brown paper wrapping, lay at her feet.

Emily picked up the basket, wondering what it held. She'd heard no knock at her door. She returned to the kitchen and tore the brown paper from the bundle.

"It's food!" she exclaimed, unable to believe her eyes. "It's food."

She found a small bag of sugar, another of flour, and went on to pull out vegetables, cheese and bread.

"Where did this come from?" she asked herself. "Whose is it?"

Then softly in Emily's inner thoughts came a beautiful scripture verse: "My God shall supply all your need according to his riches in glory by Christ Jesus."

"Thank you, Lord," breathed Emily. "Thank you." And she set her basket on her kitchen table and sank to her knees at the nearby chair.

"Forgive me for doubting, Lord," she wept. "I should have known you had it all under control—all the time."

And Emily carefully portioned out the food that had been

provided. It would do her for many days to come if she used it sparingly.

But the following week, another food basket appeared on Emily's doorstep.

I wonder who is bringing them? she pondered. *Someone is certainly an Angel of Mercy.*

All through the remainder of the long winter, Emily continued to get weekly supplies. None of her congregation knew anything about the baskets when she shared with them her wonderful provision. Emily had thought that it might be Sophie, though she knew Sophie was hard pressed to care for her own family's needs. Then she wondered if it was Carl. He was always watching out for her. But Carl was just as surprised and excited as anyone when he heard the news. The Reillys were not bringing it. They would have brought it openly had they known Emily was in such need, Mrs. Reilly told her.

Others too were surprised that Emily had been so low on provisions.

"But the cookies?" asked Mrs. Cummings. "You always had store-bought cookies."

"That was all I could afford," admitted Emily. "I just didn't have enough money to purchase all the ingredients for baking at any one time."

"Oh, my," said Mrs. Reilly sorrowfully, "if only we'd known. I can't forgive myself for allowing you to go hungry."

But Emily only smiled. "Don't feel guilty," she assured them all. "God meant it for good. I learned more about leaning on the Lord this winter than I have in my whole life. I learned the wonderful truth about faith and trusting God."

Along with the continuing food baskets, her congregation sometimes blessed Emily with a bundle of carrots, a small bag of potatoes, some canned goods or baking, an occasional roasting chicken or piece of beef, and often—very often—with eggs and milk. And, as an added blessing, the Sunday offerings increased.

———

A letter from Ruth included the news that the two new mission workers who had been approved by the district at the last conference were doing well at their postings. Verna, who had quit the year before, was now married to the grocer in the small town where she had gone to serve. He was an older man, widowed with two small children.

Emily smiled. "Imagine me married to *my* grocer," she chuckled. "Wouldn't we have one jolly time growling at each other!"

The more serious side of Emily kept her praying for Big John McMann. But she wondered if she was making any headway at all.

Emily had begun to feel a thawing on the part of his sister. Vera McMann greeted her warmly when she went to the store. And she came for tea about once a week.

Still, the woman forbade the discussion of "religion," and Emily chafed that she couldn't share the reason for her faith with Vera.

"Lord," she prayed, "I'll love her and you talk to her."

So Emily poured tea and chatted about the weather, the present wave of the flu, and commented on the news Miss McMann heard over her wireless.

At one point Emily wondered if it was she who was leaving the groceries at her door, but after some candid statements, Emily realized that the woman knew nothing about the food.

Emily's visits with Sophie and her children were bright spots in her week. They never missed a service at church. On Sundays, Sophie's sign hung boldly in her window: "Closed for Worship." At first she had worried that her business would suffer, but she happily told the little congregation that her receipts had actually increased.

One early spring day when the eaves were dripping and water was running in muddy streams down the sides of the town's narrow streets, Emily decided to don her rubber overshoes and take a walk in the woods.

It was a long time since she had visited the creek she loved, and she was sure it was pulsating with new life now that the sun had filled it with melted snow.

Dressed warmly in an old coat, Emily found the creek to be just as she had expected. Here and there, through the winter ice and snow, the stream had managed to flow southward, clearing its path as it wound among the slope of the hills.

Emily sought out her familiar log and settled herself to gaze at the blue stretch of sky above her head.

"I've made it through another winter, Lord," she breathed quietly. "Thanks to you and your care. Now we face another spring. As wonderful as it is, it is a hardship too. The mud will be deep for a while. I won't get much calling done. I do hope my garden is more workable this year—though you did get me through last winter without it. Still, I can't expect those food baskets to keep dropping from heaven forever. But thank you for them, Lord. I much prefer those to food gifts from ravens." She paused a moment and pictured her heavenly Father on His glorious throne smiling with her at her little joke.

"It's been a good year. A hard one in many ways—but I've learned much from you. It was hard to lose Nicky—but wonderful to welcome Sophie as a sister in the faith. And thank you for Mrs. Woodrow and the way she has grown spiritually since giving her life over to you. I'm sorry that I was not able to talk to Mr. Woodrow before he died. Of course, only you know what might have happened in his heart before he passed on into eternity.

"Thank you for bringing Carl here. He has been a real blessing to me. I'm glad he caught on so quickly that we can only be friends. He's such a good friend to have, Lord.

"I guess the thing that has bothered me the most—the oftenest—is the Travis family. Lord, it seems that there should be some kind of a solution to that problem. Surely someone could do something before one of the family members is hurt very badly. If I should interfere, in spite of what Mrs. Travis says, Lord, please make that clear to me.

"And then there is the matter of Big John and Miss McMann. Lord, I have failed in trying to share the Good News with them. I don't see where I have made any progress at all—though she is friendly now. Almost seems to want my company.

If you simply want to show your love to her through me, I'm willing, Lord.

"And Big John? He still growls and grouches when I come in—though he doesn't taunt me anymore about being called to preach. I'm thankful for that—I wonder if he ever checked the scriptures I gave him. Only you know that, Lord.

"And thank you for caring for Ruth—and each of the others who have gone to serve you. Be with Morris as he leaves for Africa. Ruth says that he is to be married before he goes. I never really felt he would take time to find a wife—but you work out some marvelous things.

"Be with each member of my little congregation. I thank you for the Reillys. She's been like a mother to me—and it sometimes makes me miss my own mother even more. But it's been good to have her, Lord. I love to have someone to talk with who is motherly and wise—and who has loved you for a long time. When I visit with Sophie, she's more like a sister.

"And, Lord," Emily hesitated. "Be with Shad, wherever he is. Help him to put aside his bitterness—whatever caused it— and to open his heart to you. He needs you, Lord—and I know you still love him." Emily paused again. "And sometimes I'm— I'm afraid I love him, too," she added.

Emily finished her prayer with tears in her eyes. She wondered why she was unable to forget the man who seemed to have so completely stolen her heart—but who was so wrong for her to love.

Chapter Twenty-six

The Letter

When summer arrived, Emily planted her garden after Carl spaded it for her. She hoped the absence of the weeds might encourage her seeds to grow more prosperously.

"If it does well, I'll share it with you," she had promised Carl.

"No need for that," he assured her. "Ma always plants a big garden and she sends her stuff to me already canned."

Emily laughed. "Well, I won't make any such promises," she said lightly, and thanked Carl warmly for his help.

The garden was doing much better than it had the year before. Emily counted on it supplying vegetables for the entire coming winter.

"My pa is sick." A voice suddenly interrupted Emily's concentration as she weeded her carrots.

Emily lifted her head and saw Rena standing nearby. "Sick? How?" she asked, wondering if Mr. Travis was beating his wife again.

"He keeps throwin' up and he's too weak to get out of bed," said Rena.

"Does your mother need help?" asked Emily.

"She said to fetch you," answered the girl.

"What about Dr. Andrew? Does she want him to come?"

211

Rena shook her head.

"But I can't do anything for a sick man," Emily told her.

"She doesn't want you to. She just wants your—your company," said the child, and Emily went to her kitchen to wash the soil from her hands and get a light wrap.

"Let's go," she said to Rena and the two set off for the Travis farm.

She found the man in even worse condition than she had feared. Rena was right—he was very sick. His face was sunken, his skin had a yellowish cast, his eyes were bleary and unseeing. From time to time he thrashed about the bed, and then fell back exhausted, the sweat standing out in beads on his forehead.

Mrs. Travis had said nothing as Emily slipped in by her side. Emily sat silently for many minutes and then reached for the woman's thin hand. "I will fix you some tea," she whispered, and went to the kitchen.

She took the tea to Mrs. Travis and kept vigil with her, occasionally quoting a psalm from memory in a soft voice until the evening shadows began to lengthen.

"The children should be fed," Mrs. Travis murmured wearily.

Emily left for the kitchen to see what she could find to make a meal. The cupboards were almost as bare as Emily's had been the winter before. She did find enough to make a batch of pancakes, and soon the griddle was sizzling, the smell of pancakes filling the air.

Timmie and Rena ate hungrily, and Emily continued to flip pancakes until they declared themselves "stuffed"; then she fixed a plate for the mother. But Mrs. Travis only picked at the food. Emily encouraged her to eat even though she did not feel hungry.

At last Emily removed the plate and washed up the supper dishes along with the stack that lined the tiny cupboards. After she finished, Emily prepared the children for bed and read them a story about Jesus blessing the children.

When she was sure the children were sleeping, Emily fixed another cup of tea for Mrs. Travis and offered it to her as she moved her chair beside the woman. Mr. Travis was quiet now. He had ceased to vomit and twist about. It seemed to take all his effort just to suck in another breath. Emily felt anxious and uncomfortable. Would they just sit and watch him die?

"Shouldn't I get Dr. Andrew?" she asked the woman again.

"He's been," said the woman shortly. "Nothing that Doc can do now. It's just a matter of time."

The woman reached out and took the fragile hand of the man on the bed. She stroked it gently—lovingly, and Emily couldn't help but cringe inwardly.

"Suppose you wonder how I can still love him," she mused aloud. "Well, I haven't always loved him. Sometimes I hated him—with such a passion that I could have killed him. I wanted to at times because of the way he was hurting the children."

She was silent for a while, and then she went on. "But one day I was reading my Bible, trying to find some sense to life, when I came across a verse that says that we're forgiven just as much we are able to forgive. Well, that stopped me right there. I knew—I knew that if I was to ever have peace with God, I had to forgive him." Her eyes rested on her husband's wasted form. "Even if he had caused me pain and suffering," she continued. "At first I thought I'd never be able to do it. And I couldn't have—in my own strength. But God helped me. I did forgive—and with that forgiveness I learned to love again.

"Oh, not like at first. Not like I loved the young man who won my heart long ago, but rather like a mother—pitying and caring. He was not just hurting us—but himself. I sometimes think that he has suffered most of all."

She stopped again. "And so, though I still feared him—though I could no longer respect him, I didn't hate him either. I loved—but in a different way."

Emily felt she understood. In a way she loved him, too—this broken, degenerate man.

"He'll not make it this time," the woman went on quietly, "an' it grieves my heart. For I know he isn't ready to go. He hasn't prepared to meet his Maker. There isn't one thing more I can do to help him. He's made his own choices—and he must face the consequence. I have prayed over and over that he be given one more chance—one more chance to start over. And God has answered that prayer—time and again. Now I realize that he will not change—no matter how many chances he is given." This time her reserve broke and her voice caught in her throat. "It's a hard thing to accept the truth—but—I have to give him up now. There's no use putting my children through any more pain."

There were tears falling as she stroked the still hand of the man on the bed. Emily's heart ached for both of them—for the woman in her pain and for this man who, spiritually, was already dead. She stirred in her chair and said she would see to the fire.

"God," Emily prayed when she was alone, "I've asked often for this family to be relieved of their suffering and pain—but I didn't mean this way, Lord. Isn't there another way? Is she right? Has he had his last chance?"

Emily put wood on the fire and paced the small kitchen before she was ready to once again take her place beside Annie Travis.

All through the long night they kept their vigil and into the next day. At two o'clock he breathed one last struggling breath and lay still. Emily knew he was gone. She knew that Mrs. Travis was aware of the fact also. There were no tears. The woman simply stood to her feet and drew the sheet slowly over the face of her husband.

"It's over," she said sorrowfully. "You can send for Doc Andrew. He will need to prepare a death certificate."

Emily nodded and left for town. "Oh, God," she prayed, "if he only had made his peace with you. I didn't want it to end this way. I had so hoped and prayed . . ." But with a heavy heart Emily had to face the truth that there would be no more chances for Wilbur Travis.

———

The postmaster handed Emily a letter. She gazed at it curiously, not recognizing the handwriting. *Maybe it's from one of the officers of the church telling of some coming event,* she pondered as she started for home. *It certainly isn't from anyone I know.*

Emily tossed the letter on the table and removed her coat and bonnet. Walter sauntered up to greet her, and Emily picked him up, thankful for the warmth and companionship of the friendly cat. It was so much nicer than coming home to an empty house. She put another stick of wood in the stove and pushed the teakettle forward, knowing it would soon be time to put her supper on. When she had made her simple preparations, she sat down at the kitchen table and tore off the end of the envelope.

Emily could see that the note was not more than a few lines in length. She let her eyes fall quickly to the end of the message.

The letter was signed simply, *Shad.*

Emily's heart began to pound. *What does Shad have to say to me?*

Dear Emily, he wrote, *I'm sure this letter will come as a bit of a surprise to you. You may have forgotten all about me—but I assure you, I have not forgotten about you. Aunt Moll has kept me posted on your welfare and your work.*

I missed my yearly trip to the farm and also the annual Autumn Picnic. I would have loved to be there—but I have been unusually busy.

I plan to visit the farm next weekend. Could I possibly see you? I have some things I'd like to discuss, and a letter doesn't seem appropriate.

You can send your answer home with Aunt Moll. She will be in to do her grocery shopping on Thursday as usual, and she promised me she would drop by. A simple yes or no will do— though I do hope with all of my heart it will be a yes.

Sincerely,

Shad.

Emily was both puzzled and exhilarated. *What does it all mean?* she wondered. *Shad is coming home, and he has much he wants to talk about. Where has he been, and what has he been doing? How come Mrs. Reilly hasn't mentioned him? It doesn't sound as if there's been any kind of rift between the Reillys and their nephew.*

And so her thoughts churned round and round in her mind. Emily was glad it was Thursday. She was sure she couldn't have waited one more day for some insight into the unusual letter.

When Mrs. Reilly called to drop off Emily's eggs and milk, she had a little smile about her lips. "Did you get a letter?" she wanted to know.

Emily nodded. "I did. But it was rather—rather strange. Shad didn't say where he was or where he's been. It was all somewhat mysterious. What's been happening, anyway?"

"Now, Emily," began Mrs. Reilly, "Shad made me promise long ago that I would say nothing until he felt it the right time. I guess he feels that the time is now—he's coming this weekend, you know."

Emily felt her heart pounding, but she was still puzzled. "I know. He—he asked me to tell you whether he could—could see me or not."

"And what is your answer?" inquired Mrs. Reilly.

"Well, of course I will see him," responded Emily quickly and then blushed. "I mean—I often wondered about him, how he was doing and all."

Mrs. Reilly smiled again. "When?" she asked.

"When—when will he want to see me?"

"Well, as soon as he can, I expect. He's arriving Friday. Tomorrow. Around four, I should think. He can pick you up and bring you out to the house."

"No," said Emily impulsively. "Tell him I'll meet him about—about five—by the fishing hole. He'll know the one I mean," she finished in a rush.

Mrs. Reilly smiled again and leaned to kiss Emily on the cheek. "Shad will be pleased, I'm sure. And after you've had your little talk, come for supper," she invited. "In fact, plan to come for the night. We might want to spend Saturday together."

Emily puzzled even more as the woman left the house, but she had little time to dream about what might happen on the morrow. If she was to while away her Saturday visiting the Reillys, she had to prepare for Sunday lessons now. She at once set to work, though she did find it terribly hard to concentrate.

Chapter Twenty-seven

Partners in Service

Emily did manage to collect her thoughts enough to have her Sunday school lesson and her little sermon ready. She even had a bit of time to spare and carefully washed her hair and brushed it until it was shining.

She pressed her best skirt and tied a new ribbon on her favorite blouse, then polished her worn walking shoes with the remainder of her black polish.

I don't quite know why I'm fussing so, she told herself. But deep down inside, Emily did know. Shad was coming home. She didn't know why he wished to see her, but for the moment it was enough that he did.

Emily held herself in check until four o'clock and then she could stand it no longer. It would take her only about thirty-five minutes to arrive at the spot on the creek bank—but it would do no harm if she was early. *Shad won't know of my impatience. He won't arrive until five,* she reasoned.

With burning cheeks and pounding heart Emily set out.

It was a beautiful summer day. Lazy clouds drifted loosely across the sky, looking like wandering sheep feeding in a meadow of blue. *That one looks like a horse at full gallop,* she noted. *And that one like a rose with silvery petals. Oh, now it's changing into a frog, ready to make a giant leap.* Emily laughed at her own imaginings and tried to slow her hurried pace.

"It's not proper to be so eager to meet a young man," she

217

scolded under her breath and forced herself to slow down.

The wild roses filled the summer air with the sweetness of their blossoms, drawing the honey bees to fill their cups at the waiting storehouse. Emily smiled as she watched them dipping into one flower after another.

Emily was intent on reaching the creek and sitting beneath the shade of the poplar trees so she might quiet her impatient heart and control her emotions before Shad arrived. But to Emily's surprise, Shad was already there and waiting in the very spot where she expected to gain her control.

"Hello," she greeted him shyly. "It's been a long time."

Shad stepped forward and took her hand in his. "It has," he said, looking deeply into Emily's shining eyes.

He released her hand and led her to the place where he had spread his jacket on a fallen log.

"Sit down," he invited, his voice filled with eagerness. And Emily was only too glad for a chance to sit.

"You haven't changed," remarked Shad rather shyly, and then added softly, "I'm glad."

Emily felt the color rise in her face. *You haven't changed either,* she was going to say. He still made her heart beat faster, her cheeks flush. *But no. No, that isn't right. There is something different about you. I'm not quite sure what it is yet, but—you seem—you seem more—more* . . . her thoughts went on.

But Shad was speaking.

"Boy, I have practiced this little speech over and over, and now that the time has come to make it—I don't know where to start."

Emily looked at him with questions in her eyes.

Shad ran a hand through his thick hair and laughed nervously. "Well, I guess the best place to start is at the beginning. So much for prepared speeches."

He laughed again and reached for Emily's hand. She did not withdraw it, even though she wondered at his action.

"Remember when we first met?" asked Shad, and Emily nodded slowly.

She didn't suppose she would ever forget.

"Well, you—you impressed me. The way you took my teasing. Your seriousness over your call to the ministry. But at the same time—to think of you as the—the preacher in town made me—well, I felt mixed-up and angry.

"You see, my father had been a preacher—and at one time I thought that I would be a preacher, too, and then my mother got sick. Really sick—but there was no money for a doctor. We watched her get weaker and weaker every day."

Shad paused, the memory still very painful on his face.

"And then, without warning, we lost Dad. He had been the strong one—but he was gone—suddenly—with a heart attack. There was no money, no pension, no place for us to live. We had to move into a tiny two-room shack, and I watched as Mother's health continued to fail."

Emily's eyes misted. She could well imagine the pain of the young boy.

"Well, I decided if that was the way God took care of His preachers, I wasn't going to be one. And I told Mother so in no uncertain words."

He paused again.

"Uncle George and Aunt Moll heard of our situation. They came and got us both, and we lived with them until Mother's death. As soon as Mother was gone, I headed for the city and a job that would care for me in my old age.

"I had a good job—when I met you. But I wasn't happy. And there you were, a little bit of a girl, struggling with the work of running a church. I knew that if I—and other young men like me—hadn't shirked my responsibilities, you wouldn't need to carry all that weight alone.

"It bothered me. But I tried not to let it show. Instead, I had the crazy idea of wooing you away from your calling.

"Well," he smiled softly at Emily, "that didn't work either. You put me in my place, in quick order. And I also realized that if it had worked, I would have been terribly disappointed in you. I guess I wanted you to be stronger—more committed—than I had been.

"But I still couldn't get away from the fact that you had been true to your calling and I had turned my back on it. It bothered me—day and night.

"At last I decided to do something about it. I wasn't happy anyway. I might as well do what I had been called to do.

"So I made things right with the Lord and set off to do what I should have done in the first place."

"You mean—you mean—?" asked Emily.

"I quit my job and went off to train for the ministry."

Emily's eyes grew big.

"You're a minister?"

"Not quite. I still have some more schooling ahead."

"Oh-h," murmured Emily, her voice barely audible.

His grip on her hand tightened.

"What will Aunt Moll say?" wondered Emily.

Shad laughed. "Aunt Moll has already said everything there is to be said," he told her.

"She knows?"

"She has always known. Aunt Moll has sent regular packages of cookies and toilet articles. She said that they were more than happy to have Mother's prayers answered and her son in the ministry—where he belongs." He blinked quickly several times. Emily tightened her grip on his hand.

"Aunt Moll never said a thing to me," she said in a puzzled tone.

"That's because I asked her not to."

Emily was shocked, and her expression told him so.

"I wanted to be sure," he explained. "Sure that I was going into the ministry for the right reasons. Because I had a call—not because I had a crush."

Emily felt her face flush again.

"And do you have a call?" she asked softly.

"I do. I'm sure of it now. God has confirmed it in a number of ways. I don't feel worthy to serve, but I am willing to give my life to it. He will need to take me—and use me. I'm nothing in myself."

Emily smiled. "That's the best news I've ever heard!" she exclaimed. "No wonder you didn't want to share it in a letter."

Shad released her hand and stood to his feet. For a moment he watched the swirl of the creek water. A dragonfly dipped for a water bug. Above them baby robins quarreled in the nest over who would get the proffered worm.

"That isn't what I didn't want to write in the letter," he said slowly.

Emily's eyes widened. Shad reached for her hand and helped her to her feet.

He was very close to her. She could feel her heart pounding. She felt she should move back to get some room, some perspective, but she was rooted to the spot, not wanting to move away.

"What I couldn't write in the letter is the—the fact that I care for you, Emily. Deeply. You have both my respect and my—my love. I was hoping—praying—that you might find it in your heart to honor me with permission to call—to write when I'm away—and perhaps, if God wills it . . ."

Emily's breath caught in her throat. She wondered if she was hearing him correctly.

"Could you—would you, Emily?" he asked huskily.

Emily wanted to answer but she couldn't find the words.

"I know this is sudden—that I have no reason to think you care at all for me—except—except the look in your eyes long ago when you told me that you'd pray. Have you prayed, Emily?"

Emily nodded, still silent.

"Has God answered?"

"Oh-h, oh, yes," murmured Emily with deep emotion.

Shad reached out to take Emily by the shoulders. He looked searchingly into her hazel eyes.

"And the answer?" he prompted.

Emily swallowed. Tears formed in her eyes as she looked steadily into Shad's. "It—it would seem the answer is yes," she whispered. "God has called you again into His ministry. And—this time you are choosing obedience. I—I have never had a prayer answered more—more fully." And Emily's eyes shone with the marvel of answered prayer.

Shad smiled and pulled her into his arms.

"I'm so glad God answers prayer," he whispered, and Emily blushed.

"Oh, but I didn't pray for this," she protested hastily, drawing back, her face red at the thought that Shad might think she'd prayed for his love.

But Shad quickly silenced her. "I did," he said softly as his arms closed about her, holding her tenderly, his cheek against hers. "I did. If God so willed."

And Emily smiled softly to herself as her arms lifted slowly to encircle his neck.